DANTE OF THE
MAURY RIVER

DANTE OF THE MAURY RIVER

GIGI AMATEAU

CANDLEWICK PRESS

To OTTBs and people who love them

✱

Copyright © 2015 by Gigi Amateau
Frontispiece illustration copyright © 2013 by Lindsey Windfelt

First edition 2015

Library of Congress Catalog Card Number 2014945450
ISBN 978-0-7636-7004-7

15 16 17 18 19 20 BVG 10 9 8 7 6 5 4 3 2 1

Printed in Berryville, VA, U.S.A.

This book was typeset in Horley Old Style.

Candlewick Press
99 Dover Street
Somerville, Massachusetts 02144

visit us at www.candlewick.com

For where your treasure is,
there your heart will be also.

Matthew 6:21

CONTENTS

CHAPTER ONE

JUST BREATHE

Come on. Breathe."

Those are the first words I heard in my life. I had been foaled just ahead of spring, in a deep freeze of winter. Arrived on a night when the world outside was encased in ice and the world inside was draped in dark.

Most Thoroughbreds are born in April or May, after the snow has melted and the ground has thawed. But the truth is, birthdays don't mean all that much to most horses.

Oh, getting here early by a few months can give a racing colt or filly a boost during that first year. Early foals, like me, will likely be bigger, stronger, and faster than the later babies. After that, the actual date of birth matters not a hill of beans nor a field of hay. Nobody remembers, after a while, whether you were born in winter or spring or any other season, because once the New Year rolls in, we Thoroughbreds reset our birthdays to the first day of January.

For the record, I came into the world during February. February fourteenth to be exact. Way early for foaling season, but there's always an early one.

I can still recall the pause between my first breath and the next. Quite a disruption, for sure. An entire universe of wonder and beauty between breathing in and breathing out. A full-on leave-it-all-on-the-dirt meeting between inspiration and expiration.

"Breathe, breathe," the man yelled at the moment of my entry into this world. To be honest, I didn't understand a lick of what he was saying or have any inkling what he meant for me to do.

I could feel his tired skin pressing against mine, and I felt his heavy breath hovering over me.

"Let's get his heart going," he said, but I couldn't figure out to who-all he might be speaking. Everything was dark.

He kneaded my chest, then he jibbed and jabbed at my heart, and that hurt.

Up till then, I had only ever known the warmth

and protection of my dam, but now I felt an icy wind through the shed's thin walls and it chilled me to the bone.

I couldn't figure out what was happening, but I got this much: something was going wrong.

"Come on," the man begged again. He crouched low and massaged my chest with his palm. Pounded on me hard. That hurt, too, but I was helpless.

The man spoke directly to me. "Twenty-five years ago I attended a delivery on a night exactly like this one. A colt. Your grandfather, Dante's Paradiso."

Marey stirred in the corner, but I was far from her in body and moving on in spirit. She whickered. "Please. Your family needs you. Don't give up. Breathe. Give me one breath."

"Breathe" made sense when Marey said it.

I took exactly one, just like Marey asked me to do. Then instead of grabbing for another, I turned around back from where I had come, searching for that sweet, lush limbo where nobody had to tell me what to do because there everything was open and natural and free. And there, I was part of everything.

Though I had a powerful yearning to stay with Marey, I had an even stronger one to leave my body behind. Even before life was fully mine, I longed to go somewhere else.

"Try," Marey whispered toward me, motionless.

* 3 *

I drifted away not because I didn't love her but because I felt a stronger pull beckoning.

"You are destined to follow your grandfather. Please, just try, son. Please."

She nickered softly.

Then, I expired. Let it all go.

I bounced between light and dark, cold and heat. A golden net lit up the barn and wrapped me in its folds. My spirit hovered above the foaling floor, watching the effort to revive my body below. Steam curled up from that new little black colt lying on the cold ground. Groping hands reached out to rub life into me. The man bent over my chest, but not even his sharp breath could pierce the cold pall around my heart.

✳ CHAPTER TWO ✳

BLOODLINES

The distant sound of hoofbeats lured me from the cold foaling shed. Along a broad, starlit pathway that stretched out at my feet, Thoroughbreds from my bloodlines across the ages surrounded me. Upon my word and honor, I testify that I knew each one by scent and sound even though we had never met. These ancestors warmed me with their own breaths and led me through land and water and sky.

Honest to thunder, I didn't even consider staying in that hard frozen place. I stood happily among my pedigree, amid a brilliant rolling landscape far beyond the foaling barn back in Kentucky.

Now, some might say I'm getting a tad carried away in my imagination, but consider this: we all possess ancestral memory. Every one of us knows and remembers places, faces, words, and triumphs of spirit and flesh that we have not lived but that, somehow, we know to be true. Knowledge and memory come to us through our bloodlines. And that's a fact.

I had left my dam and my body behind, refused to take that second breath, and, in doing so, transitioned from a dim place to a brilliant one. While the vet worked to revive my body, and while my dam rested in the corner nickering quiet encouragement, I walked alongside my dam's father, my grandfather, the first Dante. Dante's Paradiso.

"Why am I here?" I asked the stallion.

"You've arrived now because the pedigree needs you," Grandfather Dante replied. "The breed needs you. This is the time for a new kind of champion, but you must conquer three great tests. We're all counting on you."

"What if I fail?"

Grandfather Dante snapped his tail against my barrel. Then he touched his nose to mine, and my heart twitched. The smell of damp grass on his muzzle made me remember Marey.

The horizon in his world was swathed in emerald

and violet-gray grass. Grandfather Dante and I, both as black as night, stood together under the golden stars. "I don't want to go back," I confessed.

"You are precious to me," he said, "but now you must return to Kentucky. You have important work to do for our breed. Return through the bloodlines whenever you need me."

"But how? How do I get back to Marey, and how do I come here again?" I asked.

"Use your heart" was all he said.

"Wait! How will I know what to do?" I pleaded. "What are the three great tests?"

He nuzzled me once more, and I thought I might break open from loving my grandfather so much. Then, he was gone. The sky turned black, and I heard a whinny, then a nicker.

I opened my eyes. My nostrils closed shut, then surged open wide. Pushing, shoving, rubbing, coming from every which away.

"Open your eyes!" the same man as before yelled.

I refused.

I tried to turn back, but Grandfather Dante was gone.

"Breathe!" Marey exhaled, and I breathed her in.

Before I could even attempt to stand, someone pinned me down. Others jammed my hind with needles.

I thrashed around and kicked out into a chorus of "Ow. Ouch. Wow, he's strong."

"Had enough?" the man asked me.

Oh, I kept kicking. Believe me, even as a newborn I was strong enough to inflict mild suffering on unfriendly hands.

"I'll tell Mother we should call this one Dante's Inferno." The man half laughed. "Okay, fill him up with milk. Fill that little belly up till this guy drops off into la-la land."

While they held me down, I whinnied for Marey, and when I did, one of them pried open my mouth.

"Outstanding work, everyone. Now, pay up. Each of you owes me twenty-five dollars. If you check the date in our live-foal pool, you'll see that I had today, February fourteenth, as the date we'd see our first live birth."

"What?"

"Are you for real, Doc?"

"Oh, I'm for real. Pay up."

"You're actually going to make us cover you?"

"Absolutely. You do realize that your employer breeds Thoroughbred racehorses, right? Betting and winning. That's the name of the game."

"But he hasn't stood yet."

"Was that the bet?"

The young woman with the bottle stroked my cheek. "Don't worry, little guy. You'll wake up near Mama. Shhh . . . close your eyes."

For sure, I was born a horse in conflict, and conflicted I would stay for a mighty long time.

CHAPTER THREE

A GOOD SIGN

My expedition to the ancestral plains and back—whether real or imagined—surely did wipe me out. All my kicking and fighting; plus, the milk that got poured into me didn't exactly help to rouse me, either. When I finally came to, it was morning and Marey was standing over me, nibbling behind my ear and whispering, "Son. Son. Wake up, now."

I opened my eyes, and realizing exactly where I was and where I wasn't, I closed them again. I was desperate to be grazing in the golden field alongside Grandfather Dante. Instead, there I lay on a soft bed of shavings, the sunlight pouring in the stall window, and a cloud of Marey's sweet breath rolling over me. Some colts would've thought they'd died and gone to heaven. I had already done exactly that, though, so I knew the difference.

"Can you stand yet?" Marey asked me. "Rise to your feet. You must be standing square, with your legs straight, and moving around when Mrs. Eden comes."

I've learned that mares love to boss other horses, people, or any living being in their vicinity. Can't help it; they're born that way. They're only trying to pass along knowledge and learning as fast as they can, because a broodmare never really knows when her foal-rearing job will end. Here one day, not the next. But that's the way of all horses.

In bossiness, Marey was no different from any other mother. Every time she opened her muzzle it seemed like she aimed to set me straight with some dire, critical wisdom about something I'd need to know sooner or later.

I only wish I had listened.

"Up, up, up," Marey said.

The truth is, exhausted from being born, checking out, then coming back, I didn't much want to stand. But, from the way Marey was nudging at me, I didn't figure I had much choice, either.

Shoot, I figured if I couldn't go back to the brilliant green fields to graze and run with Grandfather Dante,

I was as happy as a snail right where I was. The sun washed softly over me, and tiny flecks of dust and shavings swirled in the air around me, almost like stars.

"Who is Mrs. Eden?" I played for time.

"The fine horsewoman who runs Edensway Farm, our home. She cares for all of us. She's the one who bred your grandfather, my father, Dante's Paradiso."

My dam lectured on about my being an Edensway foal. "The whole world is yours, all waiting to see how the grandson of Dante's Paradiso will go. How far? How fast? And how high? To get anywhere, however, you must first stand. Now."

Marey was the boss of me, so I got to my feet.

Somehow, I managed to push myself up onto all fours, right as the matriarch herself entered the barn.

"Good morning, everyone! Thank you for your efforts last night." She greeted the interns and staff in the foaling barn. Unbelievably, she actually thanked them for the mounds of pain they had inflicted on me. "I hear from Doctor Tom that you saved the colt's life. Thank you. Thank you all."

She came closer, and instinctively, I backed myself into a corner. With not so much as a knock or a greeting or a peek, she burst into the stall and held her hand out toward me. "Come on. Stand beside me."

Funny thing is, half of me wanted to obey without

question. But the other half won. I shook out my mane. Wobbly though I was, I pawed the floor. A warning.

Go over there so they can hold me down? I thought. *Force another cold, hard tube down my throat?* Never would I let that happen again.

"Well, look at you," Mrs. Eden said. "My gracious, holding a grudge? A beautiful attitude it is, too. I'm thrilled as can be to live to see this day." She reached her hand toward my cheek like she owned me. I reckon she did. I snaked my head left and right. The fine horse lady just stood there, waiting for me to stop flailing.

"There, there. You're fine," she said. "No more worries. The worst is over. By far."

Then Doctor Tom showed up, and so I reared up.

No lie to say I wanted revenge on that one. Not only had he poked and prodded and beat my heart to life when I was perfectly happy elsewhere, he had ordered a whole group of his underlings to force-feed me till I passed out. The man couldn't be trusted. I wedged myself into the corner, looking for protection.

"See what I mean, Mother? Mean as a snake."

"And gorgeous. Who does he look like, Tom?"

"You know who. Spitting image of Dante's Paradiso."

All their attention made me nervous, but my dam stood right next to me, nickering and nuzzling me.

Mrs. Eden spoke again. "Come on, little one. Let me see you. You're a gorgeous boy. That I can tell."

Marey stepped toward the lady, and she urged me to follow along beside her.

"Good boy," Mrs. Eden cooed. "My son, Tom, here, is the one you ought to worry about, not me."

"Gee, thanks a lot," Doctor Tom said. "He and I got off to a swell start last night."

Then Mrs. Eden stepped directly into my space, but before I could warn her away, she tickled my chin right where it itched. Then she rubbed my itchy-twitchy nose in exactly the same way that my dam had been all morning. And so, for a moment, I closed my eyes.

"Mister, my son saved your life last night. Did you know that? You left us for a few good minutes, but your doctor wouldn't give up. Partly because he wanted to win the live-foal pool, but mostly for me."

"For you and for me, Mother. I know how you loved Dante's Paradiso. He's the first horse I remember. I loved him, too."

A little bitty person came running into my stall. I tried to pull away from Mrs. Eden's hold, but she was as strong as a fence.

"Hi, Ya-Ya!" the child said. "No school today because of the storm. I can help in the barn!"

"Well, good, Melody." Mrs. Eden offered her cheek

toward the child. "Kiss, please." Straightaway, the girl kissed her grandmother, then me.

"Daddy, is this the foal you told me about at breakfast? You were right. He looks like the painting of Dante in Ya-Ya's study and the statue in the driveway."

"Yes, indeed. This guy acts more like Dante's Inferno than Dante's Paradiso though. Ya-Ya's trying to make friends with him. Think you could help? He seems to like you."

I did like Melody already. She was smaller than the other people and newer. She sparkled when she saw me, and she smelled sweet, like nothing I had known before.

Melody turned her back to me and pulled a shimmery-shiny something out of her pocket. I had to see exactly what the girl was fiddling with, so I walked right up to her shoulder and peered over.

"He's curious," said Mrs. Eden. "That's a good sign. He's interested in Melody's chewing gum wrapper."

Doctor Tom made a face. "Oh, he's got a spirit of inquiry, no doubt. Got it in spades."

Mrs. Eden smacked him lightly with the back of her hand. Had she popped him good and hard, I'd have made her my friend for life.

"You know what I mean, Tom? He's bright. He's paying attention. He's confident; the look of eagles, I'd say."

"Uh-huh, and his legs are crooked," said Doctor Tom. "Oh, joy. More money."

I had angled my head to the right to keep watch over these new people. Mrs. Eden's eyes traveled down my chest to my legs. I thought of trying to kick her, only as a warning. To make it known, if I hadn't already, that I didn't really care to be messed with. Not even by a fine old horsewoman.

I remembered what the helpers said the night before while I was kicking them. "Strong. Powerful. Fiery." Nobody had said "crooked."

I twitched my stifle just a smidgen, testing the lady, for sure.

Mrs. Eden eyeballed me. "Don't even think about it, mister."

Her sharp tone delivered its own quick kick, so I danced around but figured I'd best keep my feet to myself. All four of them.

"He may look like Paradiso, but I foresee trouble. That's my prediction for this one," said Doctor Tom.

"Nonsense. Paradiso was a spirited colt as well," the Edensway matriarch retorted. "Both of them fierce. You know, you're right about the name, though, Tom. We'll call him Dante's Inferno."

Mrs. Eden crouched on one leg to get a look at mine. I could knock her over. Easy peasy, I thought. Then my dam nibbled at my neck to distract me. "Stand still," Marey urged me. "They're almost done."

The horsewoman's hands traveled up and down my cannon bone. "I see what you mean. Genes. I'm beginning to think that every blasted colt and filly from his sire, Prince Firenze, shows crooked legs. Let's remember that for the future."

Melody asked, "Ya-Ya, is it bad that his legs are a tiny bit crooked?"

"Oh, a good deal more than a tiny bit. Still, that's a flaw of fashion more than function." Mrs. Eden held out her hand, reaching for Melody's help in standing. She slipped her fingers in her pocket, pulled out a mint, and opened her palm to Marey. "Thank you, Beatrice, for bringing us Little Dante."

Doctor Tom sure was determined to pester me. He refused to let it go about how my legs looked. "Mother, is it even a question? A stooge could see that those legs aren't even close to honest. We'll send him to the clinic. Let them decide whether to scrape or screw. He'll come back straight."

"Of course that's what we'll do, if nature won't fix itself in a week or two. He's our top prospect for September. We're under a microscope with this first foal out of Beatrice. Yes, we'll fix his legs when the time comes, but I don't have to like it."

She reached the stall door, then said to me before leaving, "We're all rooting for you. The good Lord knows racing could use a star like your grandfather. And I'm counting on you, so we'll do whatever it takes, my friend. If success means surgery for you, then so be it."

CHAPTER FOUR

THE TRIPLE CROWN

I was beginning to understand that everybody at Edensway Farm was counting on me to do *something*. I had yet to comprehend exactly what that something might be.

After Mrs. Eden, Melody, and Doctor Tom left, I swallowed hard and looked up at my dam. "What is everyone counting on me for? I'm just a colt, Marey."

"Son, here at Edensway, there's no such thing as *just* a colt or just a filly. Our people made their fortune from breeding Thoroughbreds to race. My father, Dante's Paradiso, is still the most famous racehorse in the world, even though he is gone now. Twenty-two years ago this June, he won the Triple Crown of racing, and no horse has done so since, nor beaten his times on those tracks."

"What is the Triple Crown?" I asked her.

"The greatest sporting event of all time, consisting of three races."

"Three tests? Three great tests?"

"Tests? Why, yes, that's a way to think of it. A jockey and a horse race together. Sometimes, running so fast and hard that they court the grave. Sometimes, death is the real victor of the day. Three races, run in May and June every year. Each track presenting a different question: Are you fast? Are you powerful? Can you endure?"

"And Grandfather Dante, was he fast and powerful?"

"Everyone, the whole world over, agrees that he was!"

"And did he endure?"

"Like no other horse before or after! He had an enormous heart. And I suspect you do, too. Since such things come from one's mother."

"Marey, why are you so nice to Doctor Tom and Mrs. Eden when they always bother us?"

Marey pulled some hay from the fresh flake beside her. While she pondered her answer, I nuzzled close under her, right where her downy winter coat smelled like milk.

Finally, she answered me. "The Edens are our

family, that's why. Mrs. Eden remembers my sire. So does her son, Doctor Tom. They miss him because they loved him very much, and he loved them, too. Just like we do."

"I only like the little girl. She's nice."

"Shhh . . . you mustn't say that. You're only here because of them."

"Well, I do love you. And Grandfather Dante."

"You mean you love hearing about him."

I shook my mane hard. "No, *him.*"

"You can't possibly love a horse you don't know. Not many people and even fewer horses remember my father. I myself was a yearling when he foundered. I recall once when he was led past the yearling barn. He stopped and turned to look right at me. I lived in the same stall—the one reserved for the top foal—that he had lived in. A tradition you'll certainly continue. Anyway, that day he nickered at me as he passed by. I cherish that memory."

Of course I had met Grandfather! Hadn't Marey ever visited the ancestors, like I had?

"But I did meet Grandfather Dante and all the rest of the ancestors."

"Is that so?" Marey asked. Marey was the first mare to confound me, but she was not the last.

"Yes, on the night I was born. First, I heard Doctor Tom telling me to breathe. And then, I got up, walked

across some stars, and met Grandfather Dante in a field. He let me graze beside him, and he nickered in my ear, too."

Marey tilted her head to get a closer look at me. She nuzzled my neck. "My tired colt. Take some milk, curl up, and get some rest."

I was getting pretty riled up that everyone around me was always trying to get me to drink milk and go to sleep. Nothing doing till I convinced Marey to believe me. I met her gaze and shook my mane hard this time. "Really, it happened the way I told you!"

She nodded and let out a sigh. "True, you didn't breathe for a very long time last night. I thought—I thought I had lost you. Doctor Tom gave you a shot of Adrenalin to jolt your system. I could only hear what was going on around me. What you experienced was most likely a hallucination. A kind of dream. I'm sorry, darling, but you didn't leave the barn. I know, I was praying over you the whole time."

When she tried to wrap her neck around mine, I pushed her away.

She whickered. "Good glory, you've had a busy day. The air is getting cold in here for a newborn." Marey pulled some shavings into a big pile. "Come on, my February boy, I'll keep you warm."

The bedding sure did look inviting, I admit. The harder I tried to stay awake, the drowsier I got. But I

wouldn't lie down. I needed to make my point. I surprised myself, and Marey, too, with how hard I stomped my foot.

Marey stepped back. "Calm down. You're headstrong like him. I believe you experienced *something*, little racehorse, but I don't know what."

There was no purpose in fighting my dam or the sleep that was coming on strong. I moved closer to her and flopped right down, near enough to soak in the warmth from her body and deep enough that the winter wind stalking the cracks in our stall couldn't catch me.

Though I'd have to wait two years to run my first race, my mind was already racing with thoughts of conquering the three great tests and becoming a champion like Grandfather Dante.

CHAPTER FIVE

THE GRAND PLAN

One morning, while I was napping, a ruckus as loud as I don't know what startled me awake. Usually, nobody was up and about during quiet time. Doctor Tom and Mrs. Eden were particular about giving Marey and me time to rest and bond. They liked everything to run predictably, day in, day out. Sticklers, Marey called them.

The hooting and hollering of the crew jarred me right into attack mode. No lie about fight or flight; that's how it is with us prey animals. I shut my eyes tight and kicked out so hard in all four directions that I splatted right down on the floor when I landed.

"Glory, son," Marey scolded me. "Learn to welcome the sound of our people feeling happy. We like those noises."

I opened my eyes to find Doctor Tom and Mrs. Eden gawking at me. Double trouble. I stumbled to my feet and backed into the corner, pretty sure one or the other of them was packing a hypodermic with my name on it.

Doctor Tom said, "Let Beatrice settle him down. She will. He's a challenge to be sure, always pacing and snaking that big head of his."

When will they realize? I wondered. *No one is going to needle me without a fight!* I scraped my hoof along the ground.

"Now, watch. Here he comes with the head again," said Doctor Tom. "Chill, little guy. You're already famous! Like your mama and your granddaddy."

"Here, Tom." Mrs. Eden held out her hand. "Let me see the magazine." She stayed quiet for a good long time. Everybody did. Then our matriarch smiled and nodded. "I'll read it to you. All right, here we go. From the March issue of *Kentucky Bloodlines*:

DANTE'S BEATRICE DELIVERS PRINCE FIRENZE COLT

The first foal out of Dante's Beatrice, two-time Horse of the Year, winner of the

Oaks and the Breeder's Prize, was born February 14 at Edensway Farm. Edensway representatives confirmed that Beatrice delivered a son of Darley sire Prince Firenze. According to Edensway Farm president, Anita Eden, the jet-black colt is the spitting image of his grandfather Dante's Paradiso, who won the coveted Triple Crown twenty-two years ago this year. Edensway Farm executive vice president and farm veterinarian, Tom Eden, said the colt came earlier than expected and it was a difficult delivery for Beatrice. Mother and son are doing well. When asked what the colt is like, Mrs. Eden said, 'Precocious, gorgeous, and powerful. And he doesn't like Tom!'

Doctor Eden added, 'He went to Hades and back to get here. He's still not happy with me. Here's the good news; he has Dante's Paradiso's large heart, thanks to his mama. We're pleased with the colt. He's fiery and strong, and we couldn't be happier.'

Edensway Farm released this photograph of Beatrice and her son, nuzzling in their private paddock. They have not decided where the colt will go in September."

When Mrs. Eden finished reading, everyone cheered. Marey arched her neck and pranced in place. My proud dam nudged me up toward the stall door. "No fighting, son. This is your moment. No one here wants to hurt you. Trust me."

"I just wish they weren't so loud," I said. "Now is the time I'm supposed to be resting, and you should be eating your hay. I don't like all of this fuss."

"Hush, hush, now. You need to learn one thing: you and I live under a watchful eye that will never close. You heard what Mrs. Eden read. The entire racing world is waiting. Your father has already proven himself worthy of continuing the bloodlines. He has sired several champions. You're my first. They want to know if I'm a good mother."

"Oh, you're a fine mother, all right! And I'm a good son."

She nickered into my ear. "They want to know if you will be a great racehorse. They're looking for signs."

"They?"

"The fans. I have a lot of fans and so do you, already."

"Will I be a great horse?"

"Your pedigree says so, for sure. Your family tree includes grandmothers and grandfathers who were among the finest racehorses in history."

"And you, too!"

"You're right. I was a very good racehorse, faster than your father, even."

I shook my mane and nudged her shoulder. "What is racing like?" I wanted to know.

"Oh, very hard work. The race goes off in a flash, after days and days of training and practicing. Horse and jockey learn to work as one. I loved my jockey most of all."

"Did you try to win one of the three tests?"

"I did," she said. "I won the first but came up short in the second, finishing fourth, just out of the money." Marey nudged me playfully. "I met your father at a big track in New York. He posted to the inside, and I drew up beside him. Racing is in your blood, as sure as the sun is shining on your poll right now."

Marey was right. The sun was shining into our stall and washing right over me. The morning air carried sounds from the pasture of broodmares ripping out grass from the earth, and foals whinnying across the fields.

Almost springtime. Too good to be true and too sweet to last.

My break from Doctor Tom didn't last, either. He came back later in the afternoon with a halter for Marey and a smaller one for me. Now I had to be on my guard. Best to keep alert and ready to defend myself.

"No funny stuff, little star," Marey said. "Watch what I do, and do what I do. Start learning this lesson now: the easier you are with people, the kinder they treat you, and all the better your life."

Marey lowered her head right into the halter that Doctor Tom held up. When he stepped out, she moved with him. On the contrary, one of the interns started tugging on my lead before I could even try to mind my manners.

"See, Marey? Did you see them yanking on me?" I asked later. "All of them, they always come around with injections and pointy things, or if they don't, they're pulling on me, and it hurts. I don't like being hurt."

"No, they're trying to help you. You have to trust that sometimes even something you dislike can help."

"I hate shots."

"They keep you healthy."

"Those ones who come to take my blood? They hurt me today."

"Most foals don't need three people holding them down in order to draw blood. I hope you were nice to them. Were you?"

I turned away and pretended not to hear.

"Oh, no, don't tell me. Did you kick out again?"

I considered fibbing, but Marey already looked disappointed. I nickered softly as I tried to explain. "They don't act nice or gentle. They don't ask or warn me or anything. They poke me as if I'm not even there, like I have no feelings. I don't like needles. Not how they look and not how they sting."

Marey tilted her head toward me and angled her eye right up near mine. She peered way deep into me, the way she sometimes did when a cricket landed in the water tub. I didn't dare move away.

"What?" I finally asked. "Are you looking for something?"

She swung her head across the grass and aimed her muzzle at the sprouty dandelion leaves. "You're a different sort, son. I've never known another like you."

I walked away to get out from under Marey's gaze.

"Oh, glory." Marey whickered after me. "Come back. I need for you to cooperate. The Eden family is judging me by you. You nearly died, and that's on me."

I spun around to face my dam. "Nearly? I did die! Mrs. Eden said so."

"Whether you died or not, Edensway Farm is a business. Doctor Tom and Mrs. Eden have spent more time and money to get you here alive than either of us can understand. They fret over economics, those two. You and I, we are their future and their security."

"Is that why Doctor Tom pulled me out of the ancestral plains?"

"Precisely why he wouldn't give up on you, yes. And because he is a good man who loves horses."

"A grouchy man who likes to bother me."

"Have I not already said this? Get used to being bothered. Anyway, you return the favor and then some." Marey sounded harsh.

"He's the pest, not me. I only protect myself."

I looked down at a spider crawling across my hoof; her legs tickled me.

"Isn't that bug pesky?" Marey asked.

"She's not hurting me."

"Nor is she helping you. You don't blow her across the paddock, yet you could. Why are you so angry with Doctor Tom? Have you ever seen me bite, kick, or head-slam anyone?"

She had a point there.

"Son, I want you to start imitating me. I'm not asking you; I am giving you a command."

"Marey, I will try."

No more coddling from Marey. "You'd better do more than try. With every action and every reaction we are borrowing against or building up our futures. Both of us must be successful in order to have good long lives. No choice."

Marey snapped me with her tail. She had my full attention. "Listen to me. Your entire life was planned out for you before you were born, before you were even bred. Down to the amount of water you will drink and the kind of feed that goes into your bucket."

"My whole life? Everything about me?"

"Everything. So you might want to wise up and get with the plan."

I looked around the pasture. All the fences were painted white, and the fence lines were clear of brush and weedy plants. Even the empty fields were trimmed and neat.

"Marey, but I didn't arrive as planned, did I?" I knew I was as right as the sun. "I was born different. So maybe I'm supposed to be a different kind of Thoroughbred. Did you ever think about that?"

Marey stood as square and stiff as the life-size statue of Grandfather Dante out front. "No," she huffed. "The best thing for you, me, and this farm is for you to do as you're told, so that you can be sold at the best September sale."

I reckoned everything was running exactly according to the grand plan to get Edensway back on top. Everything except me.

CHAPTER SIX

WATCHING AND WONDERING

Over the next few weeks, more fillies and colts were born. Mrs. Eden paid me regular visits to check on my progress. She spoke freely and with no shame about how there was money to be made and a reputation earned from selling the right foal to the right sheik, prince, or oil tycoon. The matriarch wanted the entire crew to know that any one of her new horses could end up worth millions. She also knew that any one of us could be worth nothing. Nothing's exactly what she was scared of. I appreciated her honesty.

What I needed, if you'd have asked me, was to play with Marey and the foals of Kentucky on those graceful bluegrass hills outside the foaling barn without everybody watching me. With so much at stake, it was all eyes on the mamas and the babies, at all times.

Believe you me, Mrs. Eden was all business about getting us foals ready for September. I heard her and Doctor Tom discussing which ones of us they thought they might send to Lexington's prestigious Thoroughbred foal sale. Every dam hoped her foal would represent there.

Mind you, if you pay attention to what all's going on around you, you'll hear an assortment of interesting facts. For example, I once heard Marey and the other dams remarking on how the barn doors needed painting, how the mats in the stalls could use replacing, and how few barnhands were left working at Edensway. "Not like when we were fillies," they said.

The severity of money trouble meant that every hand available was needed. Even those of a child.

I was grateful for the mischievous presence of Doctor Tom's daughter, Melody, who befriended me for the while that I lived at Edensway.

Melody resembled a miniature version of her father. Long and lean. Both of them redheaded. And with lots of it. Hair, that is. Doctor Tom had a bushy chin, and Melody, a choppy forelock that fell down past her eyes. Her father frequently brushed his hand across her face and teased, "You need a haircut."

She'd swat him away. "I can see fine, Daddy." Then she'd add, "You need a shave." She was fiery like me, I remember.

I do believe the youngster liked hiding behind her hair. Same way as how I sometimes hid behind Marey or squeezed into the corner of our stall. Just to have a welcome minute to myself.

At nine years old, little Melody was one of the best handlers I've ever known. She had collected a lifetime of horsemanship skills by then. Observation being chief among her talents and one that is often both sorely absent and undervalued by grown men and women.

Now, if I sound harsh, just remember this: a horse is a prey animal. As such, we spend our entire lives observing. We're not out there just eating grass, but always watching and wondering what's next.

My point here is that Melody was not a prey animal but a predator—as are all humans—yet she proved herself to be a true friend of the horse. Skills learned at the knee of her grandmother, a legendary figure in Thoroughbred racing, and her father, too, I suppose. He is well respected by many humans and horses—though admittedly, I was a latecomer to the Doctor Tom fan club, and more of a junior member, anyhow.

One morning Melody plip-plopped herself onto

the fence and started eating her apple, ignoring me like I was as natural a part of the landscape as the redbirds that liked to nest in the thick old clematis climbing up the back of the barn.

Though small and relatively new to this earth — compared to, say, Mrs. Eden — Melody possessed a good pedigree for horsemanship. But she could only handle me because I let her, and she helped her cause aplenty by not once in the entire span of time I knew her ever approaching me with a needle in her hand or anyplace on her person.

My first groom didn't so much mind the switchover to Melody. Let's just say that he and I were of opposing minds about how I should be treated. I observed that he was as scared of me as the field mouse is of the red-tailed hawk. No reason to get into all that, though. No sense in embarrassing a novice. I'm sure he went on to find success with a milder, calmer, slower Thoroughbred foal than myself at a different farm.

Melody, of course, never met a colt or a filly that frightened her. "We should keep him," she suggested to Doctor Tom one day.

"There's a lot more involved in that than what you might think," he replied.

"You're talking about money," she said.

Wise child. Moolah and marigolds almost always drive these sorts of decisions.

What I didn't quite comprehend, despite Marey telling me over and over, was that to whom much is given, of him much is required. An important lesson right there. One I wasn't keen on learning, either.

CHAPTER SEVEN

CROOKED

Just when I was about ready to forgive Doctor Tom for inflicting every blasted procedure onto me, he outdid himself. I heard these frightful words resurrected from Red, one of the few remaining nonfamily employees: "Look how crooked them legs are, Tom."

Marey snapped her head up fast, like thunder chasing after lightning. Then she caught herself and looked over at me with droopy eyes, acting cool and standing calm, as if nothing were wrong. She was faking it.

I thought the world had agreed that crooked legs were more about fashion than function, but apparently not.

"Just try to be good," Marey said, because she knew a nightmare surely was headed my way. A halter. A trailer. And a long ride, but not to Lexington.

Sure enough, Doctor Tom had me carted away from Edensway without Marey and without Melody. All by my lonesome, I traveled to a clinic where I met dozens of colts and fillies, every last one of them with crooked-leg syndrome, like me. If it even really was a syndrome.

The lot of us was there to have our little foal legs broken and reset straight. Or if not broken, then every last bit of the crookedness scraped off. Either way, I could see it coming: a world of hurt.

Oh, I fought them. Yes, sir. Why, I had a reputation to uphold.

I kicked and bit at the white coats coming toward me. Struck out, twisted up, and went buck wild. I never considered, not even once, Marey's plea to surrender.

Not a single man or woman succeeded in getting me down on their own. I gave them a wild and wondrous show of brawn and bravery, till a whole gang of them banded together.

They surrounded me. Some I could see, and others tucked themselves away into my blind spots. I kicked out sideways with all my might and all four of my feet.

No go. One of those rascals sprung out from nowhere and injected me with a tranquilizing serum as powerful as two bellies' worth of milk.

Yes, my archenemy, the needle, brought me to the ground.

It packed a hullabaloo of a punch that right quickly taught me the whole, full, and true meaning of surrender. Down I went to my knees.

Some hours later, I awoke feeling puny, with my front legs wrapped tight and throbbing. No idea what they'd done to me or even how they did it.

Within a day, Doctor Tom reappeared and got me onto the trailer without any hassle. Of course, I was fuller of medication than I was of myself. That helped his cause, but only temporarily. I just hadn't had a chance to reload. And the truth is I was glad to smell bluegrass hay in the trailer, same as the kind I loved at home. Home is where I wanted to go. Back to Marey and Melody.

The ride ended at Edensway, where one of Doctor Tom's interns walked on the trailer to lead me back into the foaling barn. She tugged on my halter. "Here we go. Let's get you back with Mama." We walked slowly to the stall I shared with Marey. I could hear her whinnying for me.

A welcoming party of family and friends greeted me — Mrs. Eden, Melody, and the whole team, including Doctor Tom. I knew I needed to set Doctor Tom straight once and for all. Who knew what sinister plan he might concoct next?

My back legs being the only good ones available to me at the moment meant I had to lure him in close but not too near my backside. I lowered my head and feigned the thing everybody wanted from me: surrender. Doctor Tom took half a step, and I walloped him hard in the shin. No lie, I would've nailed his other leg, too, but he jumped out of the way.

"Holy crap," he complained to the intern. "That really hurt. Here. Let me have him. This colt needs to learn his lesson."

He took my lead from an assistant. His anger zipped along the rope, but I wasn't scared of him.

"Dante!" Melody burst into my stall and threw her arms around my neck.

Doctor Tom lightened his grip.

"Poor colt," she said, and stroked my neck, then nuzzled my face. "Oh, I missed you so much. I worried about you every day." She looked up at Doctor Tom. "Will he be okay? When will the leg wraps come off?"

"He's going to be just fine, sweetheart. You know how I know that?"

She nodded. "Because he's happy to see me."

"You got it. He wasn't happy to see me, though. He kicked me!" Doctor Tom said.

Melody giggled.

"Not funny!" Then Doctor Tom's callused hand rubbed my cheek.

* 41 *

"He sure likes you. And he trusts you. I think you can help this colt even more if you want to. Lord knows, if he's going to have a good life, somebody has to help him figure it out."

Mrs. Eden spoke up. "Tom, don't be so melodramatic. You've seen plenty of good horses with bad attitudes. The great ones are worth it."

Doctor Tom just nodded.

"You're not letting me off the hook, are you?" he said to me.

He appeared to be waiting for something from me. I didn't lower my head, but I didn't go after him, either.

"I know you want to be in charge, buddy. From here onward, every turn your life takes will be because of a choice you make." Doctor Tom sighed.

He ran his fingers down my front legs and lightly squeezed the wraps. "Looks like they did a real nice job," he muttered.

I was trying not to hold a grudge and, even harder, not to head-butt him. I will admit that I wanted revenge something fierce, but I loved Marey, and she had asked me to try to be a better foal.

Doctor Tom released his hold, and I went straight to Marey, who nuzzled my poll. I thought she also might want to kick Doctor Tom, so I tucked under her hind. But she didn't pin her ears or show him angry eyes. Of all the surprises in the paddock, she whickered at him. Like she was thanking him.

"Son, you look well," my dam said. "I'm glad to have you home."

"Marey, I hardly remember a thing, and what I do recollect is the worst pain."

"Oh, you'll know worse, believe me." She whinnied right in my face.

"What's funny about that? And what do you mean?" I asked.

"Little Dante, Kentucky is your birthplace. Mine, too. And your father's and grandfather's. There is no finer place to claim, but you won't stay here forever. You'll travel the land, training and racing. Such a life is not for the weak. Some days every ounce of your body will long to lie down. Every cell will ache and throb and beg you to stop. Your lungs will burn; your heart will beat so fast you will think you're going to collapse, and you might. Or you may make your name and future on the track and return here to live a long and good life, if you do everything right. Right now, that's a very big IF."

In a most loving way, my dam continued, "Something needs to change, son. Please. For the family. For the bloodlines."

"But, Marey, I've done everything you've ever

asked me to do. You asked me to stand, and I stood. When you wanted me to walk and run, I did those things, too. When you tell me it's time to sleep, I sleep."

She popped her front hoof hard at the ground. "Trust me, I know all about the burdens that a foal of your pedigree carries. I was one! The pressure on a broodmare is even higher. I'm tired of begging you: act right. Got it?"

I looked away from Marey to far across our pasture. My own heart beat loud and strong in my ears. Out on the farthest hill, I imagined seeing my grandfather again. His head tilted and his eye gazing upon me. I imagined, also, how happy everyone would finally be when I was the next Triple Crown winner. I rubbed my face against Marey's belly, then looked toward the horizon.

"I will, Marey," I promised. "I'll make the bloodlines proud one day."

The next morning before turnout, Doctor Tom separated my dam and me. He came to get me himself and walked me down the yard to the weanling barn. And of all things, Marey let him. She bowed her head and closed her eyes, like she knew all along.

CHAPTER EIGHT

FRESH START

Awhole bunch of us got moved up the hill: me and nine others, including my chestnut first cousin, Covert Agent, who got himself sent to the crooked-leg clinic not too terribly long after I did. Covert, by a different sire, out of Marey's sister, Gemma, was also a grandson of Dante's Paradiso. He was a little dusting of a fella with a lot of heart.

The new place was a good bit larger than the foaling barn. All ten stalls aligned down a single lane. Each had its own door and a white column, all situated in an orderly fashion and connected along a finely masoned breezeway. Our rooms opened toward the Edens' old, sprawling brick house, out of which came some sweet, sweet smells on Sunday mornings. Sugar, Honeycrisp apples, and I couldn't tell you what all else. Trust me, I had no trouble learning to linger around my stall door on Mrs. Eden's baking days.

From the front, I gazed out over the life-size statue of Grandfather Dante. The driveway wound past our barn and down the hill to the foaling barn and the paddocks and the turnout pastures. There were other barns over that way, too, for stallions and retired mares. I never saw inside any of them.

At the new place, each of our stalls shared a grated half wall with its neighbor, and we'd all get to cribby-crabbing at each other over any little piece of news: feed, hay, visitors.

I lived right next to the feed room in a stall that had always been reserved for the best foal, like Grandfather Dante and Marey before me. Across time and history, the imprint of every prior top Edensway prospect permeated the walls, the air, and everything about the space, and that's what gave my stall an aura unseen by human eyes. Wisdom, confidence, and knowledge emanated from the wooden walls surrounding me.

Inside there, I enjoyed a welcome plenty of space to stand and turn and pace about if my supper ran late in arriving. Looking out the back window, I could gaze across the entire north acreage of Edensway.

From there, I kept an eye on my old paddock, the broodmares, and the newest foals. Sometimes in the very early morning, I spied on Marey way down that hill, but when I whinnied, she never picked up her head or even called back to me.

Despite the comforts afforded me, the move away from Marey and into the status-stall tested me greatly. I didn't care a lick for all that change.

CHAPTER NINE

A Peace Offering

In the new barn, it was just us colts and fillies. Nothing but a bunch of young wild things figuring it out for ourselves. Heck, by then I must've weighed five hundred pounds, easy peasy. Maybe more. And, shoot, I stood taller than more than a few ponies. So I sure didn't look that much like a baby anymore.

At first, I figured I'd enjoy not having any mares nearby to boss me around. I learned pretty quickly, though, that also meant no Marey nearby to explain how things worked, to nuzzle me when I got confused, or to show me how to act brave.

One saving grace was that Doctor Tom brought Melody to visit straightaway. She herself was like a filly, in some ways. Long gangly legs, a branchy neck, and a full mane that fell well down her back.

I was standing in a paddock, turned out with Covert, when the two of them came over to check on how I was settling. Doctor Tom placed a hand on Melody's shoulder. My halter and lead rope were looped over her other one.

Next thing I knew, Melody tucked both her hands in her pockets and giggled. *That's trouble,* I thought. I sniffed the air and caught a sharp, crisp scent. Something familiar to the nose but foreign to the tongue. Not rich like early morning grass. Not savory dam's milk.

She held her hand out flat. I walked over to check it out. "Peppermint. For you!"

Then she popped the treat into her own mouth. "Or, for me!"

Melody always was a little old prankster of a girl. The confounding thing was that neither Doctor Tom nor the child made any sort of move to catch me. No harping or chirruping. No kissing the air. No staring me in the face.

I would almost say that neither flashed any interest in haltering me at all. Except here Melody came again, and wafting through the air was the intriguing smell of peppermint.

I casually wandered over and grazed near the girl. She turned her back to me, all the while tinkering with that spiffy-sniffy morsel in her hands. Unable to help myself, I snuck up behind her and very lightly touched the back of her arm with my lip. Doctor Tom stepped in close by me, too. Naturally, I moved a step back. He spoke softly. "How about a fresh start between us? For real this time."

Well, I about froze.

Was Doctor Tom calling a truce?

On instinct, and from having formed a habit of rearing up and kicking out at Doctor Tom, I shifted my weight. Just to collect some power at the ready.

The girl extended her hand again. Perched in the middle of her tiny palm: one round candy about the size of my nostril. I pondered over whether to smell it or to eat it. The promise of sugar and mint and potential goodness dissolving in my mouth? Mmmm . . . mmmm. I closed my eyes and breathed it in.

"For you," she said, a second time. "Really truly." The faintest quiver ran across her open palm; her stretched-out fingers nudged the scent toward me. "Go on. Take it."

So I did.

In a soft wave, she folded her hand along my neck, right where Doctor Tom and his students preferred to draw blood and stick needles. I tensed but didn't bolt because next she scratched my mane at the instant of its itch.

Besides, Melody wasn't armed. She had no weapons on her; not a needle or syringe or thermometer in sight.

The girl rubbed my neck and chest and muzzle in the way Marey often had. That memory triggered a wistful sigh. *I am no longer Marey's foal,* I realized.

I stood still for a very long time, till my eyelids felt so heavy that I could hardly keep 'em open.

"Look at that," Doctor Tom said. "You've 'bout got him to sleep, Melody."

"Daddy," she said. "He's my favorite colt I've ever met. Why don't you like him?"

I *knew* it! I perked my ears. This I had to hear straight from the doctor's mouth.

"Oh, who says I dislike this wild fella? He's strong. He's handsome. He's got that large heart from his mama. You know she's my favorite. As colts go, I actually like him very much. Maybe Dante doesn't like me."

"Well, I like you, Daddy." Melody cocked her head and scratched my cheek in another itchy place. I leaned into her hands. "You and L.D. should be friends now. Look at him. He's so friendly," she said. And quite convincingly, too.

"I don't know that I'd use that exact word: friendly," Doctor Tom said. "Little Dante — L.D. — doesn't know it, but what he wants is to win enough to position himself to stand at stud for most of his life. That's the goal. I'm beginning to worry that his antics and his attitude might overshadow whatever standout assets run in his blood. The last thing he wants is to have to make his name by racing. That's a life, all right. A tough one. Besides, whether or not we're friends is not up to me. Everything from here on is up to him."

Melody shook her head. "Uh-uh," she said, then clucked her tongue. "Being friends takes two, Daddy. Even I know that much. Have you ever tickled his ears like this? Or, wait. I know—" She plunged her hand into her peppermint pocket, retrieved a candy, and handed it to Doctor Tom. "Here. You try."

I nuzzled her for defending me.

He smiled at her, but closed one eye and peered at me. "Hmm. What do you say? Water under the bridge?" He placed the candy in the well of his hand and clenched his fist around it. By then, I had decided there was about nothing in the world that I savored as much as the first shock of peppermint on my tongue followed by sweetness in the crunch. And there was easy pickings right in front of me, even if the prize was hidden.

I dropped my nose toward Doctor Tom's hand; he unfurled his thumb. "For you," he said, and uncurled his fingers. "Really, truly."

Now, I didn't lollygag. Just swiped the treat and nodded for more.

"Well, I'll be," said Doctor Tom. He gentled his hand and touched my cheek softer than ever before. And without a needle in sight.

Melody encouraged him. "See? You're doing great. Maybe L.D.'s just super-duper sensitive. I think he worries a lot. Maybe you have to reassure him. You know, talk to him. Make sure he knows you like him and think he's a good boy."

"Hmmm . . . could be," said Doctor Tom. "Most Edensway foals seem born knowing we're on their side. Not him, though."

Melody looked at me, then at him. "Horses are like people, Daddy. You have to take the time to get to know each one. I learned that from you."

Doctor Tom breathed in a slow breath. I breathed out. He touched my withers, then my shoulder, then my chest. No needle, no tubes, no halter.

"Seems maybe I've forgotten some things I should be remembering. What else have you picked up hanging around the barn?"

The child was a confident speaker, that's for sure. She didn't hesitate to school her father in equine matters she knew to be true. "When I was six you told me this: 'Never get yourself into a position of girl versus horse, Melody, because a horse will always win.' "

"True enough," said Doctor Tom. "A pearl that holds true for man versus horse, too."

"And when I was seven you said: 'You can't demand anything from a horse. You have to earn everything through trust. That takes time.'"

"I said that?"

"Yep. And one more thing."

"What's that?"

"'It works best when you and your horse want the same thing.'"

All of a sudden, Doctor Tom stepped back, away from me. Just when I was starting to think I might like him a little, he spooked.

"Well, my foot," he said, more to himself than to Melody or me. "Now I see these last few months a little more clearly." He knelt down to Melody's eye level. "Tell me something. When do you think I stopped knowing all of these very important lessons?"

Melody shrugged. "Ever since you bred Beatrice last year."

"Might be. This black colt certainly is our best hope at keeping Edensway going. His dam was one of the finest at the track. Prince Firenze is no slouch either. The whole racing world was watching Beatrice's pregnancy, and they're watching this little guy, too. I hope she's as good a breeder as she was a racer. If she is, we might turn this thing around. Been a tough few years."

The child blocked the sun with her hand. "L.D. is the most important horse we've ever had, isn't he?"

Doctor Tom nodded. "Well, he is right now, for sure. I won't lie. What we really hope is for Beatrice to be the most important horse we've ever had. Little Dante's got to at least get her off to a good start. Either by bringing the right price at Lexington or by burning it up on the track. Or both!"

For the whole long time that Doctor Tom and Melody and I stood together in the pasture, I tugged at the grass and hoped for more candy. After a silent little bit, the girl took a deep breath. "Everything will be okay. I know it will."

"Melody, this colt and I have been at odds from the start. You know, he died the night he was born. We delivered him, he took a single breath, and then nothing. No pulse, no respiration, no blood pressure to speak of. Dead for three full minutes. I couldn't let him go, because without him, we had no future. So I worked on him nonstop. Begged him to breathe. Rubbed his heart, his head. Did everything I knew to do. One by one my staff started to walk away. I knelt on the foaling floor and wouldn't give up."

"You saved him, Daddy."

"I know I did, baby doll. You've got me wondering if I was selfish to interfere with nature like that. Greedy, if I only brought him back to fulfill our hopes."

I walked over to a thick patch of grass nearer to Doctor Tom. He was right in some ways. I hadn't wanted to leave the ancestral plains where I could run and graze with Grandfather Dante.

But listening to Doctor Tom talk quietly about Edensway Farm, about Marey and me and the life he had built around horses, got me thinking differently. I realized that without Doctor Tom, I wouldn't have had a single day or night with Marey. Wouldn't have ever known her. Or little Melody, either.

I considered whether maybe the needles and poking and prodding were what had let me be here with my dam. I wondered if, maybe, that was enough. I nuzzled Doctor Tom's pant leg.

Melody caught her breath in surprise. "Look, Daddy! He wants to be your friend."

"I see that," said Doctor Tom. He cupped my muzzle gently in his rough hand. "Let's start over," he said.

I whickered, and Melody did, too. I shook my mane, and the girl did, too. Doctor Tom laughed at us both. "Well, okay!"

Too bad I didn't realize what all I had at Edensway. It wouldn't matter if I had, though, because none of it was intended to last forever.

CHAPTER TEN

GREAT EXPECTATIONS

Every morning I kept up a practice of watching the main doorway and listening for the singsongy voice of Mrs. Eden. "Have a good day, sweetheart," she'd say to send Melody off to school. Soon as I heard that door slam, I'd get to dancing around, because I knew breakfast was coming, my favorite meal. The barnhands would always set my grain and hay aside for Melody to dispense. When she'd appear with that bucket of sweet feed in the morning, I knew turnout was coming, too.

We foals, we'd all get to kicking at our stall doors and whinnying when feeding time was near.

A struggling little sprout of a friendship had started to emerge between Doctor Tom and me. He could see how being in the company of Melody affected me. No big mystery to me as to why.

She expected me to be a baby as I was a baby. Nothing more and nothing less. The great predictions of everyone else dissolved around her. Not that I always kept quiet and calm for the girl. She liked games as much as anybody I've ever known. And, well, I liked games, too.

Here's a snappy memory to help me explain. I can picture Melody standing at the fence, near the paddock gate, Doctor Tom beside her with Covert Agent's halter on one shoulder and mine over the other.

Father and daughter talked quietly with each other and watched me graze.

"Think I can catch L.D.?" Doctor Tom asked Melody.

"Nope." Melody shook her forelock. "You'll never catch him."

"You know, I almost gave Covert the top stall. In some ways, he is really the top foal this season."

On cue, of course, my little chestnut cousin trotted up to Doctor Tom and slipped his head right into the waiting halter.

"See what I mean about how pleasant this guy is? That goes a far piece toward making an impression on buyers. Hey, Little Dante," the vet called out to me.

"Why don't you emulate Covert, here? At least in front of the Texan who is coming next week."

That should've been a clue that something was a-brew in the barn. I hadn't yet figured exactly what, and even if I had, right that moment I was more of a mind to keep messing with Doctor Tom.

I stopped grazing and stared at his face, planning all the ways to evade him when he started toward me with the halter. He handed Covert over to Melody.

"You ought to at least take some grain," she suggested. "He is not easy to catch. For you."

A gusty fresh breeze lit upon the field and whisked my tail in the air with an invitation to mischief, as only a Kentucky wind can do. Truly, it was too beautiful a morning to come inside. I took an easy trot away on down the hill.

I pricked my ears. *This could be fun*, I thought.

"Oh, shoot," said Doctor Tom. "He heard you."

Melody giggled.

Doctor Tom followed me for a few, then looked back at Melody. Now, it would've been powerful fun if Covert would have pulled himself loose and together we could have really run Doctor Tom through the gauntlet. Run him into the corners. Zigzagged him around the paddock a bit.

While Melody held his lead, Covert stood in one spot eating grass, paying me no mind.

That's okay. I was enjoying myself even without Goody Four-Hooves, Covert Agent. I dropped my head, but only pretended to graze. I'd just have to trick Doctor Tom with Melody's help, instead.

I kept my left eye on him and kept my right on the paradise before me. Those bluegrass fields of my birthplace rolling out into forever and ever, with white fences here and there cradling Thoroughbreds of all ages and every color. That made for an easy choice of which way to go.

The fun of catch-me-if-you-can lies not in never getting caught but in persuading the man holding the halter that he most certainly can catch you, and then not letting him succeed until he's convinced himself that he can't. What a thrilling game, waiting until the last second possible—till right when the wanting hand and open halter almost touch your nose—before bolting away down the hill. Repeat, repeat, repeat. Invigorating.

I went along for a good little bit, making Doctor Tom jog after me every which away and loose. Melody on the fence, barely holding Covert's lead, cackling. Delighted. Shouting "I told you! I told you!"

Eventually, the game ended with Doctor Tom's surrender. He admitted defeat. "Okay, you win." All I ever wanted.

Melody hopped down, and Doctor Tom held his hand out for Covert's lead.

She called me over. "Little Dante, come here." I lifted my head and did like Marey always did. I craned my neck toward the halter.

"Of course," Doctor Tom said.

The difference was that Melody imagined what it was like to be me. Before opening the gate and leaving the field, she told me exactly what would happen next. "See? We're going up to the barn. Daddy needs to weigh you to make sure you're growing right. Then, I'll bring you straight back here with your friends."

Doctor Tom never took the time for small talk.

Not every horse needs such support, but every horse needs something. Somehow, the child knew what all to do because she took time to consider what I needed.

In retrospect, I have to wonder: how would my life have turned out if I had taken Doctor Tom's advice and acted a little more docile like my cousin, Covert Agent? That, I will never know.

CHAPTER ELEVEN

TIME'S A-WASTING

Life in the weanling barn was easing on toward a good routine when chaos descended. Trouble started with talk of the Texan, and then Red showed up at our part of the farm. We weren't accustomed to seeing him around anymore. Of course, we'd all known him when we were babies, so when he came sashaying down the breezeway, we let the news be heard that he was disrupting things.

The filly two stalls down from me got to kicking. She started the colt next to her whinnying, then Covert Agent and I joined in, too. Bing-banging at the doors, cling-clanging on our feed buckets. Wean drama, for sure. But the real ruckus had yet to arrive.

Doctor Tom was in the feed room when we started our impromptu riot. He gave Red a hard time. "Red's been scaring the daylights out of horses since I was a schoolboy. That right?" He laughed and clapped Red on the shoulder. You could tell he liked him.

"I'll tell you what, Dante. Red's going to be spending part of his time up here with you all from now on. We've really got him running around."

Red spoke up not to me but to Doctor Tom. "As long as Edensway's got jobs for me to do, I'm happy."

The barn was alive with the smell of Gala and the promise of Golden Delicious that morning, thanks to the light breeze that rustled up scents from the orchard straight in through the back of the barn. Mind you, we really got to kicking and neighing once the smell of apples reached us. All of us declaring to Red in unison, "We love a crisp Kentucky morning. Let us out. Time's a-wasting!"

But Red had come up the hill with a purpose. A real whopper. "Got to get you youngsters ready for the sale next week," he said. Then he hollered to Doctor Tom, "Every one of them going?"

"I think so." Doctor Tom popped out of Covert's stall, wiping his hands on his jeans. I guess he was getting himself a lot dirtier now that he was working more jobs around the farm.

He pointed toward me. "Maybe not Dante. I've

got a private buyer flying in from Houston tomorrow noontime to look at him. Let's shine him up. Make sure he gets his shots and shows well. Nothing I'd like better than to close the deal in thirty minutes and put our friend here on a chartered plane by suppertime."

He started for the feed room, then stopped and addressed me directly. "Can you cover me that spread, Little Dante? One half hour."

Right then, I really knew I wasn't Marey's foal anymore. The moment had arrived for me to step into the limelight and do right by my dam, my pedigree, and the Edens.

I nickered at Red and Doctor Tom.

"Woo-hoo!" said Red. "I'd say that's a yes."

The Texan and me started out fine. Right on time the next day, he pulled into the drive. He had come alone. No assistant. No children. No trailer and no driver.

Don't know why, but I expected the buyer from Houston to be a bigger man. Had he been a horse, he'd have been a pony, unless you count the extra height his hat gave him. Even then, he would've been riding the horse-pony line.

Doctor Tom addressed him as Junie. Red called him "Yessir." Those first few seconds held a lot of promise that a deal might get done.

Junie carried with him a shiny silver suitcase that he set down in front of my door. I craned my neck to investigate and tried to get a whiff of whatever might be concealed in there. Wondering if maybe Junie had brought me a peppermint all the way from Houston.

Doctor Tom wasn't inclined to dillydally. After all, our agreement only covered thirty minutes. So, Red clipped on my lead and walked me out. I might've done a little dancing, but not much.

"He's sure pretty," Junie said. "Black as tar, not a speck of white."

"Great looking," agreed Doctor Tom.

"How 'bout I take some measurements, Tom?" he said, and didn't wait for permission.

Junie knelt down to that interesting hard silver case. He opened it up, and I stepped back. The Texan began to piece together a real monster of a stick. He called it his measuring stick. I called it Trouble. I trotted sideways and back.

Junie grabbed ahold of my halter. "Steady, now. Steady." His grip was full strength and full-on.

"He don't like new things," said Red.

"He also don't appear to be a very intelligent animal," Junie replied.

Now, a half hour wasn't nearly up, but was I going to let him get away with insulting me like that? Not a chance. I started pawing and scraping my front hooves along the ground. First my right, then my left. Wanted to let him know I meant business and that I possessed the agility to go with either a left or a right kick. I brandished one leg, then the other.

The Texan tightened his grip on my lead, yanked my head down, and stepped in close to me. A tad too close for me to set my aim upon his shin, but I tried.

Junie didn't care for my behavior a lick. "What else have you got to show me, Tom? This colt isn't all I'd hoped he'd be."

I didn't cover Doctor Tom his half hour. The appointment didn't take anywhere near that long. Red took my lead while Junie packed up his stick. I danced and trotted right back to my box and sputtered my great relief to be done with Junie.

Before my door was shut tight, Doctor Tom piped up: "How about I show you a different colt with even more potential than the black one? Great breeding, big heart. Also a grandson of Dante's Paradiso."

"What color is he?" Junie asked.

"All chestnut."

"No white?"

"Not a speck."

Junie rubbed his palms together. "I do love a redhead. Let's get a look at him."

Covert Agent accepted the measuring stick and Junie's hard grip without a stammer. In return, Junie stroked a smooth check for seven figures to Doctor Tom. Looked like my cousin was now the top foal of the season. Not me.

CHAPTER TWELVE

STAND AND WATCH

I'll be a crossbreed if pretty soon after Covert left, every one of the remaining foals in my barn didn't get loaded up and hauled off to one September sale or another.

All I could do was stand and watch. Helpless, moving toward hopeless. The only colt or filly left in the barn? Yours truly. Little Dante.

Marey was the first one I thought about, and it made me sad for her that I was a disappointment. I looked out over my stall door, hoping maybe there was a private trailer waiting to take me to Lexington, too.

"You're not going, so whatcha lookin' at, Boss?" Red said to me. "Not to any of those fancy sales. This mess is your own doing, I'm afraid. Lucky for you, the Edens are old-school. Every now and again they keep ownership over a foal for themselves."

He scratched my neck, and even though his hands were rough enough that he could have curried me with his bare palm, I let him. I watched the cloud of dust from the horse trailer zip down the drive. Good-bye to the chestnut filly, the bay, and the brown, and all the other colts.

"Chill, my man. You'll go away, all right," said Red.

Sure enough, my turn came.

No sooner had I inhaled my grain the next morning than did I hear Red—that hard-to-knock-down bull of a man—out in the drive, scrapping and cursing the truck. He influenced the engine with his brute force, I'm certain, and pretty soon the old rig sat idling in the driveway, right next to Grandfather Dante's statue.

Some kind of business was about to unfold. With no foal left in the barn but me, I figured I'd know soon enough, so I kept licking my feed bucket to calm my nerves, biting the plastic rim, too.

I smelled Melody's bubble gum before I saw her at my door with my halter. I knew why she'd come. Right behind her stood Mrs. Eden and Doctor Tom.

Everybody had come up to the barn to say fare-thee-well. I traded breaths with the old horsewoman, and I didn't kick or bite Doctor Tom.

Melody led me out herself. "Take your time, Little Dante. I'll never forget you. Even if you never get back here again. Which, well, you probably won't."

A wisp of my mane got stuck in the stall door hinge, and I liked the thought of leaving some little part of me behind.

Two hills away, off in the distance, I saw Marey standing in her field, watching me. She grazed alongside a freshly painted white fence in a field of tall bluegrass. She lifted her head to the wind and tossed her mane, and the most reliable light breeze in all the world — the one that starts and ends in Kentucky — carried Marey's love and good wishes directly to me.

I caught her final message by the tail. "Remember who you are. Race for your family."

I took one last look at Marey. Already her belly was starting to swell. A new foal would arrive in the spring. In the meantime, I planned to do right by my dam and by the colt or filly she was carrying.

I halted before loading in order to make one last memory of my home. Marey lifted her head, turned, and trotted down the hill. Far behind her, upon my word, I think I saw the faintest trace of Grandfather Dante. I can't be certain, but I nodded good-bye, even if only to his statue. Real or made up by my wishing mind, I was relieved to have a little something from both of them to take with me.

Melody led me up the ramp, checked on my hay net, and patted my cheek. She wouldn't let Red see her crying, but I felt those loving tears on my neck.

"Be good, L.D.," she told me. "And run fast, okay?"

Red grew impatient to get moving, but Miss Feisty wouldn't hear of it till she was good and ready.

I whinnied good-bye, and Melody ran off the trailer. Before the doors closed, I saw her bury her face in Doctor Tom's shirt. A new life awaited me, one of winning or losing or who-knew-what.

CHAPTER THIRTEEN

TRAINING CAMP

I was stuck in that slow-moving trailer for pretty near a full day. Red wouldn't know a hurry if it whinnied in his ear. I got to stretch my legs only when Red stopped to stretch his. Believe me, what Red lacked in speed he really did make up for in endurance.

Along the way, I learned firsthand that the world is a big place outside Edensway. Mountains and rivers, forests and fields, highways and backcountry roads.

On a secluded compound down one of these backcountry roads, at the first line of Virginia's blue mountains, the trailer came to a stop, and I came to train for the track.

Like Marey always told me, people have had plans for me since before I was born. Before I was bred, even. The plan was mine to follow, or mine to fail. See, my visit to the in-between, where I met my grandfather, awoke in me a spirit of questioning and left me with a sense that fate had tapped me to deliver something special for the bloodlines. "The very spit of Triple Crown–winner and legendary racehorse Dante's Paradiso," people liked to say, even though everybody knows that while horses drool and salivate as sure as the day is long, we never spit. Ever.

In Virginia, where I had come to train for a year, it was the job of my trainer, a man by the name of Gary, who was always grumbling and growling about time, to mold me into the champion I was bred to be. Presumably, he had some prior experience in this, because he was highly regarded by the Eden family. Darn near every other racing family, too, it seemed.

Gary's place in the blue mountains was a whole lot different from Edensway. For one, the barn was crowded with young Thoroughbreds. For two, all four walls were enclosed, so we looked across at one another instead of across the farm. Sure, we each had our own window facing out, and, sure, there was always something going on inside to keep us entertained.

My stall wasn't even near the doorway. I expect Gary had some preconceived ideas and speculations about me. He about told me as much when he first brought me off the trailer.

"Here you go, friend," he said as he unlatched my stall and led me into a clean, boxy space with plenty of soft footing. "Putting you right next to my office. We'll be neighbors." His hearty clap to my withers sent up a little cloud of dust. Red hadn't seen fit to brush me along our way.

At my old barn, I could look straight down the breezeway and call out to the others. They'd all listen to me and show their heads and whinny. At Gary's training facility, none of us even pretended at being friends. We knew we'd all be competing against one another in the baby races once we turned two. All of us were important yearlings from well-respected farms in Kentucky. And there was a filly from New York and a colt from Pennsylvania, to mix things up.

I observed all the comings and goings-on at Gary's. While the training farm hadn't the acreage of Edensway, the campus was tucked into and surrounded by mountains as blue as the grass back home. I could partly see the mountains from my back window, and I took a lot of comfort from the solitude and knowingness of them.

Those blue mountains were swarming with little and large critters that liked to circle around the farm, all scrounging for supper. A doe and her twins left the cover of the mountain forest every day at dawn and again at dusk. Bobcats liked to crouch up in there, screaming like a lady, most every night. I saw one once. Big cat. Terrifying.

What I loved most about the mountains was to hear the owls screeching and hooting and the warblers trilling and chirping. Sounds pleasant enough to cause a lonesome colt to fill up and nearly burst with a longing for home.

Gary's barn was swarming, too, with those stern, upright predators that had been plaguing my whole short life. People with pitchforks, rakes, and wheelbarrows. Unfortunately for them and for me, people with needles and scary instruments of every sort.

At the training farm, the days, like my life, were planned up one side and down the other. Those folks weren't messing around. Always asking questions and writing down the numbers but not really listening. All talkers, no hearers, if you ask me.

"How much grain did he eat? How much hay? Is he drinking enough water? Does he need a salt lick to make him thirsty?"

"Tick. Tock." Gary's training motto didn't include much time for listening to a colt's wants or wishes.

We had scheduled turnout. Scheduled lights-out. Scheduled exercise on a hot walker. Everything aiming toward one thing: racing.

At first, I had a tough time adapting to this new way. I worked hard all day and barely had the energy to do all that was asked of me. I never got to eat enough. Being sore became my habit of being. My back, my hips, my legs. My everything always ached.

Gary and his rank old horsemen didn't seem to give a whinny about who my sire or my dam or my grandfather was. Some of the more seasoned hands walked around like the place was theirs. They spent hours a day hovering around at my behind, doing one invasive thing or another. People have been obsessing over my temperature my whole life. No different at training.

Pretty soon, I'd had my fill of all of them. After I reared up once, to protest going out again to run, but only because I needed a rest, Gary had them put a chain over my muzzle.

"Little Dante they call you? Well, listen up. Don't matter a hill of beans to me who you were when you walked in here. I promise, you'll be a different horse by the time you leave here," Gary said to me after that.

Sure enough, the training changed everything about my body and my brain. I've always liked knowing what comes next, and at training I knew everything. Every day was the same, and eventually, that made it easier for me to act more like the horse that Marey wanted me to be.

Still, even with all the monitoring and exercising

and testing, there're twenty-four hours to the day, and that's a lot of hours to be good. After my workouts on the hot walker, I'd meet up with a fairly green young man who had developed the habit of shaking in his britches around me.

That boy was half scared to hose me down in the wash stall—the other half too scared to scrape the sweat off of me afterward. Either way, I'd most always find myself standing in my stall with steam and sweat rising off me like I was on fire. I guess I was starting to grow into my name, Dante's Inferno.

My groom's other job was to put a fly sheet over me at turnout. Gary liked to keep my coat black.

"Tall, dark, and handsome, that's for sure. Let's keep him that way." He instructed the staff to cover me at night to keep me clean, and on turnout to stop the sun from bleaching me out.

To his abounding credit, the young man tried. Oh, how he tried. Dancing around me, holding his inhales till his faced darkened. I could hear his heart beating so loud that I could see his pulse a-thump-thump-thumping in his neck. His eyes bulged, exposing the whites, and those inexperienced hands shook something fierce.

When a man is showing as so blatantly afraid, I have to wonder, *What in the world is he about to do?*

When my groom came after me . . . Let me back up

here. When my groom *charged* toward me with the fly sheet, I figured I'd best jack up my back left leg in order to demonstrate I wasn't taking any mess from him.

"Put it down," he said, and his heart beat wilder and faster. Out. Of. Control. This guy.

So, I put my left back foot down and swapped it out for the right one. Just stretched my leg out to test if I was within striking distance, should I need to be.

He put in a mountainous effort to no avail. Let's just say I eventually got bored and turned away from him. Same way a barn cat eventually gets bored of batting around crickets. The groom bolted from my stall, leaving my sheet half on, half off. And presently, it fell to the ground.

Come evening time, though, somebody different tended to me. A girl.

CHAPTER FOURTEEN

A Good Start

"May I come in?"

I blinked. Not that I straightaway invited her in, but I did give consideration because she was the first to ever ask.

I blinked again, then she did, too, and piped up with, "You gonna invite me in, or make me stand here all day waiting for Your Highness to decide?"

All right, I thought. *Let's see what happens next.* I stepped back. She entered my stall with her head down. She touched my neck, and I sensed no fear in her. Zero. A slow heartbeat, regular breathing, normal-looking eyes.

Best of all, from her I felt wonder. Curiosity. Like she wanted to know me.

"What are they talking about? You're not scary, brother. No way. Not scary at all," she said softly.

She squatted down and picked up the sheet from the floor. The same one that the morning groom had bolted from. Even the manner with which she shook the blanket clean seemed like a natural, loving gesture.

This smaller person was calmer. I was starting to wonder if the bigger a person got the more chaos they had going on in them.

She stared at me, then looked away. Before I could react, she draped the sheet over my stall door, not over me.

"Let's get to know each other." She stroked my neck. Her voice was solid, like the ground. No quiver there or in her hands. She patted my neck again and said, "Beautiful. Never in the days or nights of my life have I met one as majestic as you. Magic like midnight."

The blanket remained on the door. The more I looked at the soft, supple material, the chillier the air felt around my haunches and shoulders. She walked around to my right, making no move to cover me. "I have met many, many horses, Dante. Yeah, see? I know your name. Aren't you curious about mine? Filipia. That means 'the one who loves horses,' and I love horses like crazy."

She turned her back to me and fiddled with the

sheet. Its buckles sparkled in the dim light coming from the office where Gary and the other men were grousing about something or somebody or such and such. I walked up behind her to get a look and a sniff, because I like sparkly things, and because I thought I detected peppermint on her person. Maybe more than one.

"That tickles." Filipia lifted her shoulder to her ear, a gesture that sent me away. After a while, I came on back. She laughed again. "Okay, I'm ticklish. You win!"

She started telling me a story, and I got so busy listening that I hardly realized what she was doing. The sound of her voice and the effort she was making wrapped me up and I felt safe.

"Let me tell you about my home, Dante. I am from an island where horses roam freely. They walk straight up to the mayor himself. Some of them—the strawberry roan ponies—even belong to him. The tourists call these ponies the wild horses of Vieques. But they're not really wild. They are free. The opposite of you, Dante from Hades. Ah, you prick your ears? So, you hear the nickname they call you? Well, you are the opposite of the wild horses of Vieques. You are wild but not free."

As she whispered into my ear, I'll be honest, I tried to find a good reason to hold a grudge or at least start up a new one. But there was something honest and true about Filipia.

She and I got off to a good start. Heck, a great one. 'Course she helped her cause immensely by keeping her hands free of crops, needles, and other sharp, pointy things.

I even looked forward to her mucking my stall, so I could stand in there with her.

One day, she told me, "I know your racing name is Dante's Inferno. But that's just what the Jockey Club says. All those numbers tattooed on your lip? If I trace those numbers I can then discover your birth date and place, and also your parents' names. I could find out where you were born, though I know you are Kentucky-bred. A true Thoroughbred."

She was talking about the code that Gary had arranged to have tattooed onto my upper lip, shortly after I had arrived to train. There exists, for all Thoroughbred racehorses, a code in the form of one letter and five numbers. Get a look in my mouth, which I'm nowise suggesting will be easy, and there's the gateway to my pedigree.

Filipia stopped picking at my bedding and leaned on the pitchfork. Sounding all dreamy, she said something else. "Some people think that everything they need to know about you is carried right here." She tickled my upper lip. "But I know there is something else about you. You are special, so I'm giving you a special name. *Monkey*. Okay? When you hear that name, you can relax and come to me when I call you. That way, you'll be like the horses of my island."

After that, with Filipia taking good care of me, everything seemed to be unfolding exactly according to Gary's ticktock. That is, until they tried to mount me.

CHAPTER FIFTEEN

WORK IT OUT

Around my second birthday, Gary brought over a saddle and a rider. I should've seen that coming. After all, everybody knows Thoroughbreds don't race by themselves. Running takes two—one horse, one jockey.

I don't know what I had expected, but, sakes alive, I sure hadn't wagered that the man would fling himself on top of me without first looking me in the eye, asking permission, and coming to know me.

Now, there's plenty of respectful ways to communicate with a horse. Even if your mind can't accept the possibility that words can be understood, universal languages do exist between nearly all species.

For starters, try making a soft sound that is not a growl or a bark or a yowl. For instance, those calico cats that like to hang around barns? They can purr or they can screech. Every animal on earth knows the difference and what means what.

A respectful pause at the stall door? What a nice way to greet a horse. The equivalent of saying, "Hello! Do you care to receive company at this hour?"

These methods, combined with a good-intended heart, surely will help when approaching a horse for the first time. And, of course, planting yourself where you can easily be seen.

The long and short of it is that many men at Gary's facility tried to break me. Every one of them came at me like a twister in an open field, in a storm of force and emotion. And some of them seemed to have had anger issues.

Well, I had issues of my own.

Off, off, off. I wanted each of them off, so not one succeeded in staying on.

No, sir, I wasn't about to let a man sit atop my back who wouldn't look me in the eye. Every one of them that tried failed because they didn't care a lick about me. What they cared about was payday.

So, off they went. This went on for several months.

While winter turned to spring, the other two-year-olds went breezing around Gary's track, and I fell behind. My tick wasn't tocking.

"Dante." Gary shook a fist at me, more out of frustration, more to make a point, than to hurt me. He wasn't intending on striking. He jabbed me with his words, though, sure enough.

"You're going to have to work this out. I'm burning through exercise riders right and left. The racing community is small and people are talking. Speculating you've got bad genes. A fella down in Texas says you're a danger and that your head's not right."

Now, that made me mad. I didn't care for Gary or all that drib-drab he was spouting about the fat-cat Texan. I snaked my "not-right" head right at Gary.

About that point in my training, I surely could have used some advice from Marey. I would have sacrificed a hundred breakfasts to visit Grandfather Dante again, and that's no lie. I tried everything I could to imagine him standing there, off in the distance. Nothing doing. The bloodlines had left me to figure this out all by my lonesome.

One morning, while I was resting, good old Gary started up about my being more cooperative. Truth be told, he liked to never stop.

With his face all contorted, Gary flapped and honked like a goose. He blurted out, "You're reflecting badly on Edensway. On your mama, too, for that matter. I'll tell you what, Dante. That's a crying shame because she's a great horse. You think her foals will be much in demand if you're a fiasco at the track? The legacy rests on your shoulders, my friend." Then for added dramatic effect, he threw his hands up. "Here's the deal. I got nobody else willing to even try to break you. Nobody."

Filipia stirred behind me.

"Excuse me, sir, Gary," she said from the corner of my stall. "I can do it."

Sour-faced Gary and me, we both whipped our heads around right fast. Neither of us could believe what we'd heard.

Filipia stood well within my field of vision and paused her hand on my rear end, a good sign of respect. She wanted me to be one hundred percent certain of her location. There was nothing in her hand or heartbeat or her breath to make me think she was anything other than what she purported to be. A girl who loved horses like crazy.

"You? I doubt that," said my trainer.

She insisted. "Dante knows me. He likes me, and I like him. I'm in here every day. I can get a saddle and bridle on him with ease."

"What's your name again?"

"Filipia," she responded, with more than a touch

of annoyance. I thought about popping Gary hard with my tail, but I didn't want to undermine whatever case the girl was about to make.

"You can doubt me if you want to, but I know I can ride him. Back home, on the island where I grew up, I worked with horses all the time. My brothers used to doubt me, too. But not anymore."

"How old are you?" Gary asked.

Oh, glory. Did I ever feel her heart skip and her breath stop just then. A little quiver, hardly detectable to a less sensitive being, but an indisputable tremor.

I've never been able to tell a person's age— probably because I've never really gotten a good look at their teeth. Filipia did look fairly, what I'd call . . . youthsome.

"Nineteen," she finally said. She shrank back against me.

All I could see of her was the toe of a cracked, worn-out black paddock boot beside my hoof. Now, Gary could see her the whole time.

With those two steely, predatory eyes in the front of his head, he peered into her. Then he barked, "I'll ask you again. How old are you? The truth this time."

She wrapped her hand around my tail, anchoring herself to me. "Eighteen. I just turned eighteen, sir."

Gary grunted. He spun on his heels and shut himself up in the office for a good little bit. Filipia let out a big sigh. Her breathing returned to normal, and she kept on with cleaning out my stall.

A few minutes later, though, who's standing at my door but Gary. That's right.

"I don't know what to say. This is the craziest idea I've ever heard. What's even crazier is that I'm seriously considering a yes," Gary said.

Back he stomped to his office to hole himself up.

Filipia squealed and jumped up and down. Nobody who knew me a little would have had the courage or stupidity to make such an unruly high-pitched sound as that. Nobody who knew me a bit would have made such a fuss and explosion with their arms and legs all flying around. But Filipia knew me a lot.

By grain the next morning, it was decided. I overheard Gary talking to his assistant. "You should see her with him is all I'm saying."

No sound at all came from either man except for the shuffling of papers on that clipboard that was permanently attached to Gary's hand.

"Come on. We gotta do something." He was trying his best to recruit an accomplice, it seemed to me. That way, if this radical experiment with Filipia went south, there'd be at least one other person to blame.

Sounded to me like old Gary had run out of big ideas and reasonable options.

Even before they gave us the official word, Filipia

knew. She came bouncing into my stall. "Hey, Monkey! How are you today, Mister Racehorse?" She tugged a bit of my mane. I stomped for her to quit it. "Come on, we're a team now. Right?" Filipia lowered her head and put her nose to mine, like Marey and Melody used to do.

"You're okay, Monkey, and we're gonna be great together. Do you want to know how I can be so sure? It's like my grandma—my brothers and I call her Melon—like Melon used to tell me: 'My darling, a good beginning is half the work done.' You and I had a good beginning, Dante. Don't you think?"

Like always, whenever she was working around me, Filipia started to tell me a story about her family and her island. Like always, her voice put me at ease. "You probably want to know why I call you Monkey," she said.

She emptied a pitchfork full of soiled shavings into a wheelbarrow parked at my stall's entrance. "See, I remember when I was five, the day my daddy left, Monkey. I loved him like the stars love the moon. He cried so hard, and we all cried so hard that I worried our little house would fill up with water and float out to sea with all of us. Daddy stretched out on the orange sofa, holding his head with his hands, and I was beside him. The night was so hot inside that my legs stuck to the plastic cushions. He begged Mama, 'Please don't make me leave. I'll be a better man.' She was frying bacon, ignoring his tears and mine, too."

Nose to nose, she took my breath. How I wished I had a little something more than breath to offer her. But then again, breath is life, so I hoped maybe there was enough in our sharing that would keep her there and talking to me.

Filipia kissed the soft part of my nose. "Now, you might think that if I remember all that, my good monkey, that I remember all the bad things Daddy did to make Mama hurt enough to let loose a hailstorm from her heart. But I don't remember those things. Not all of them."

She turned silent for a good little bit. She stopped her story from growing any bigger and kept on mucking my stall. Filipia was the only one brave enough to do the work with me standing beside her.

I'll say it again: she was good. She took her work seriously. She'd hunt down every wet stain, every bit of dung, any particle that might draw flies. So in return, I tried hard to do all my business in one spot. More or less.

As she was finishing up spreading fresh shavings in my stall, she set down the rake and picked up her story. "I bet you wonder why I told you all that about my family. Okay, here's why. After Daddy left, Mama started to call me Monkey. She told me, 'You're my only daughter. You and me, Monkey, we're a team now.' So, Dante, you see what I'm saying, don't you? You're my only friend here. Not a single bad thing from before matters, Monkey. We get a new start. You and me."

She turned away, disappeared without a word or breath or good-bye.

At Edensway, my water filled up on demand. On my demand. I'd simply press my nose to a big old button and, whammo-blammo, my bucket would fill up with fresh cold water. But at the training barn, I relied on Filipia. I got used to her being gone, then back in a quickstep, ducking under the gate with the green hose folded tight in her hand.

"Ha! My monkey thought I'd left without a good-bye. Never! Here, you need fresh water. Drink up."

She leaned way over, balancing on one leg while pulling the hose to reach my bucket. Just the sound of the water curling and whirling around made me thirsty. Filipia started to wobble, and I stood right there behind her to steady my partner. I pressed my muzzle into her shoulders, very lightly, just enough to tilt her upright.

"Aw, Monkey! You love me like crazy," she said.

I nickered because, well, she was right.

CHAPTER SIXTEEN

THE KNOWING PLACE

Miraculously, Gary had indeed consented to give me one more chance. An even bigger miracle? He agreed to give Filipia exactly one chance. Just one. Desperate, I reckon.

She took it; I took it. And I'll brag right now: those crusty horsemen stood back and learned something from an eighteen-year-old girl. A tiny, baby-faced girl.

"Two days," Gary barked at her one morning, about the middle of May. "That's it. I'll allow you forty-eight hours to make this happen. We've got to make up some time. All my other horses are doing baby two-year-old races already."

I glanced up from my hay, a mouthful of it dangling from my lips. As much as I wanted that little old girl to show them up and prove herself, the fact was not lost on me that her goal was to break me.

They'd already broken my knees and set them back straight when I was shy of a month old. This breaking that Gary kept talking about involved something else. Something even more precious than my bones or muscles or any other parts at all.

Gary was negotiating with Filipia about breaking my spirit.

Even though I liked the friendship that had been developing between us, well, I don't imagine there is a horse or human or any living thing who is eager to have their spirit broken.

Because without my spirit, what am I? Just a big tangle of skin and hair and a crazy mess of bones. All mane and tail with no swish or swag.

Such thoughts raced through my mind. At least something in me was racing.

Similar thoughts must have been rolling around in Filipia's head, too. Now, she didn't have a wild spray of hay dangling between her teeth, but her eyes showed every bit as white as mine.

Gary finally snapped his fingers in front of her face. "Tick. Tock. You get where I'm coming from?" he said, then turned to walk away.

"Sir, Gary?" Filipia called after him. She swallowed a gulp of air, and I'll tell you what, I figured she was about to give up on me before she'd even started. Part of me was relieved.

Relieved I might never have to prove myself. Relieved I might not ever fail at the three tests. You can't fail if you never start.

Then Filipia surprised me.

"Sir, Gary? I won't break him. Just so you get where I'm coming from."

I thought Gary was going to blow himself right out of his boots. He turned so dark in the face from heating up on the inside. I just knew Filipia's next task would be mucking a mess of melted Gary up off the floor of my stall.

But she didn't let his fuse burn all the way down. She offered up what amounted to a cool bucket of water.

"Oh, he'll accept the saddle when we're done. He already responds to my voice. But he won't be broke. No way. What good would he be to you if I broke him? Fire isn't always a bad thing. Especially in a racehorse."

Believe you me, when I heard those words I pretty near fell to my knees and invited her to hop aboard. And I mean then and there. I tried so hard to make my mouth utter some kind of sound she might understand. My effort to say thank you came out like it always does. In a whicker.

"You'll start tomorrow," Gary said.

Off he went to his office, as was his habit. This time, though, he stopped and spun around. "Let me ask you something," he barked. "When you say he responds to your voice, are you speaking Spanish to him?"

Filipia made a face as sour as any face I ever saw. "Of course not," she snapped.

Gary looked surprised. "Oh, why not?"

"Duh, because he speaks English." Then she couldn't help but smile. "But sometimes I sing to him in Spanish. Everybody understands the language of music."

To say I was excited would be an understatement. Still, I knew I'd have to find a whole other gear, as they say.

Now, when we in the racing world talk about gears, we're talking about speed and power, but I mean something else entirely here. I knew I'd need to find a deeper, braver place than I had ever been to, except maybe the night I was born.

Filipia gently placed her palm in the broad space between my eyes, and when she did, a charge rolled from her right into me.

"Here," she said. "This is the place, Monkey. See from here, and you'll have everything you need."

I jerked awake — as if a starting gun had gone off — and stepped back.

"Yeah, you feel that, Monkey? Good."

She lifted her hand, let it hover, then tugged on my forelock. "Whatever bad things you've learned till now I want you to forget. We're alike, you and I. We're talented and beautiful, and we have to take care of our mamas."

I nickered.

"Oh, speak for myself, eh? I will tell you another secret about me. I feel a lot of pressure to work hard and to ride and to win."

Believe you me, I understood exactly what Filipia meant. I could never shake Marey's last words to me or the desperate look in her eye when she begged me to be a better colt. Or the way she sparkled like a sunbeam on Doctor Tom whenever he came into the barn. She'd pivot her ears toward his voice. She wanted to please the Edens and wanted me to do the same.

Now, here was brave Filipia saying pretty much what everybody else had been saying for my whole life.

"Here's the truth, Monkey." She leaned in close to me and breathed in my coat. "Okay, here's part of the truth. My mother and my grandmother need my help. And that means I need yours. They sent me here to live with my oldest brother and his wife and their baby. My brother sends money home, and I do, too, but he has a family now. It's really up to me. Exercising, grooming, cleaning stalls? I like the work, but it's taking me too long to earn money. I need to race. That's where you come in."

She picked up a currycomb and began to rub it over my barrel. "How do you manage to get so dirty, even when I cover you up at night?"

She touched her own forehead in the space between her eyes. "Right here," she said. "All the knowledge and wisdom and vision we need is right here. Melon calls this the knowing place, or the wisdom place. Like a place that stores up everything in the past, present, and future. Like a kaleidoscope of every bit of wisdom in the universe. So, Monkey, when I asked myself the question, How can I get the chance to race? I saw you and me at the track. You with a carpet of flowers draped across your withers. Me wearing silks. Dirty, muddy silks from running and winning."

CHAPTER SEVENTEEN

A VISITATION

I can admit now that I was anxious. Not so much from a fear of being broke but from the unanswered question of my life. Would I be able to deliver?

What Filipia wanted from me was the thing I had yet to wholly offer to either human or horse. Trust.

Up till then, we two did pretty well together, but this idea of racing together would mean turning over control to a miniature creature who, fact is, kind as she was, had those small, predatory eyes in the front of her head. I knew if I was going to succeed with Filipia, I'd have to do something else first.

Surrender. Trust her so much that whatever she asked of me, I'd gladly do, even if I was afraid. Even if I couldn't see ahead.

Somehow or another, between nightfall and sunup, I'd have to travel all the ledges and ravines inside myself and come back out willing and able to trust Filipia. One. Hundred. Percent.

That evening after Filipia left, and after the sun went down and the stars came up, all was quiet in the training barn. Besides the occasional clanging of an empty bucket against the stall wall or the soft murmur of tired two-year-olds up and down the lane, I found myself feeling flat-out lonesome.

A soft rain started up, striking the tin roof of the barn. Almost imperceptibly at first. Listening to that hypnotic *plip-plop* lulled me away off into those as-yet-unexplored places of myself.

Let me confirm right here and now: horses do dream.

We dream in the daytime, while we're awake, and at night, while we sleep. Sometimes, a dream is nothing more than a strong or subtle memory ushered in on a smell. Like how the scent of rubbing alcohol always makes a replay of Doctor Tom and his needles.

Sometimes a so-called dream is like a visit. A visit with a friend or, in my case, an ancestor.

Right when I needed him most, Grandfather Dante visited me in such a dream. Now, whether this was a waking or sleeping dream, a visit or a mirage, I can't say for sure. Whatever it was felt as real as the raindrops plinking and plunking overhead.

A visitation, let's call it.

Gary had gone on home; he lived in a cabin up at the top of the property. On his way out, he had turned off the radio and shut off all the lights, except for the one hanging from the ceiling outside his office. The air was as still and thick as a board, the usual way summer handles itself in Virginia. All the feed buckets had been licked clean, and all the horses had finally bored themselves into slumber. Nothing but cicadas and hoot owls tending to the night.

What happened next, I expect, is that I nodded off, because there I stood at the edge of a starlit path. A return invitation I had been anticipating since the night I was born.

I stepped out, this time more certain of where I was headed. Sure enough, I followed the starry trail to the bloodlines through the salty call of the sea and into a foggy wall of the hills. I grazed there until Grandfather Dante came up beside me.

Here's what the great Thoroughbred champion Dante's Paradiso told me: "Go toward the water."

That stallion liked to keep an air of mystery about him, for sure. I hadn't an inkling or a notion of what he meant.

I whickered, but Grandfather Dante left me standing right back in my stall. Or, I woke up.

No more stars. No more fog. Just a barn full of dozing fillies and colts and Gary's hanging lamp, squeaking and swaying back and forth in the breeze now blowing through the barn. By that time, a hard rain pelted in through my window. I most surely did not want to go toward the water.

★ CHAPTER EIGHTEEN ★

Break in the River

Turns out, Grandfather Dante knew exactly what he was talking about. Going toward the water was the essential part of Filipia's plan. Heck, the water was pretty much the entire plan.

If I've failed to mention there was a small river called the Willis that ran right behind Gary's training compound, well, that's because I didn't know a thing about a body of water being back there. Had no reason to until time came for Filipia to show her stuff to Gary, who protested her technique mightily.

"What in the devil's hills are you doing coming up here in shorts, a T-shirt, and flip-flops?" he demanded.

"And a towel." She waved the rag in his face.

He didn't take to folks getting too comfortable or too familiar with him too soon. By too soon, I mean ever.

On seeing Filipia, I, for one, felt something on the order of relief scurry along my spine and escape my muzzle as a whicker.

"Monkey! Come on. Let's go for a swim."

As puzzling as the whole situation was to me, I went along with the girl. Gary remained as predictable as ever by blowing a big fuse and throwing a tantrum that would have put any one of mine to shame.

Filipia didn't waiver. "Sir, Gary, looks like you could use a cooling-off swim, too. Want to come with us to the river?"

"You bet your boots I'm coming with you. This is not what we agreed to. You've got about another inch before I shut this ridiculous scam down. This is not how you break a Thoroughbred."

She went on as if she hadn't heard a word. I lowered my head. She slipped on my halter, then I followed her out of the barn down a narrow grassy path. Gary, an inquisition of one, came with us.

"You'll love being surrounded by water. The Willis is the closest thing I could find to the ocean, Dante's Inferno," Filipia said.

Her calling me by my real name, not by her nickname for me, told me that she meant business. She kept on talking while we walked, and when a rabbit tore across the path in front of us, she laughed and pointed toward the cottontail vanishing in the brush. Nothing could spook her. "So, that's all we're doing today, Monkey. Going for a swim."

The path disappeared over a low rise in the land, and for the first time, I heard the soft tinkling of the Willis River. Filipia slung her towel over a low-hanging sycamore branch. She said to Gary, "You can wait here, if you want. Or we can meet you back at the barn."

"Are you nuts? You're not leaving my sight."

"If you're sure. We'll be a couple of hours, probably more."

Gary held up his camera. "That's okay. I'll take pictures. So no funny business."

"You should take pictures. And video, too, because no one will believe you. You won't even believe you."

Through all this yimmer-yammering back and forth, I stood quivering at all the strange sights and sounds bombarding me from every direction: the white bark of the sycamore, the dark opening at the end of the path, the field of sunflowers, and the *chip-chip-chip* of the goldfinches.

Filipia patted my neck to reassure me. She didn't seem scared at all. "Ready to go for a dip?" She held my lead lightly, and we waded into the Willis. Having been enlightened by Grandfather Dante that this was the course I was to follow, I went with her.

She gave not a hint of concern that I might not follow. Hey, a horse can pop a stop on almost any movement just by deciding he ain't going forward or backward. But I wanted Filipia to succeed. Heck, I wanted her to prove Gary wrong. So, step-for-step I followed her.

Now, a river is a beast of many manifestations. Never the same from one moment to the next. Like horses. Like people.

Where we entered that day, the water was smooth and deep. A horse's feet get tired of standing. Sure, we lay down now and again, but try lifting this body up off the ground. Awkward, at best.

But moving my weight around in the water? Light as a blessing. And even better was having Filipia there, holding on to my lead rope, swimming nearby. I filled up and overflowed with joy and relief. All the lonesomeness and misunderstandings of my life surged out. I felt strong beside her and let the Willis quench all my fire away.

Somehow, I knew what to do. Same way I knew Filipia had my best interests at heart. Same way I knew Melody wasn't going to stick me with a needle. Like how on the first day I was born, I could stand up, then walk.

Before too long, Filipia scooted up alongside me. And it hardly registered that we were, in fact, floating together—as in, she was sitting on my back and holding on to my mane. "Don't let me fall," she said. "Okay, Monkey?"

How could I let her down? When she put it that way, that I was, at least in part, responsible for her safety and her well-being? I don't know how to explain it except to say that I didn't feel like I was being broke at all. More like I was being wholed and healed and lifted.

So, there we were in the river. No saddle. No bridle. Floating or flying, and definitely both of us trusting. She asked me to walk out of the river and carry her back to the barn. Of course, I obliged.

Gary got it all on that camera of his.

CHAPTER NINETEEN

GET TO WORK

Filipia turned all of Gary's notions about horse training inside out and then some. We went back to the Willis more after that first day. Each time, Filipia hopped up on my back earlier than the time before. Each time, I didn't mind. Hard to believe, but I trusted her. Harder to believe, she trusted me.

The water soothed me. Not only did I feel an utter relief from the weight of my body off my feet, but my mind took comfort in the river, too.

Sure enough, when her two days were up, there I stood, shiny, tacked, and ready to go. Gary gave her a leg up, Filipia nudged me forward, and we walked on, easy as you please.

Gary jumped around like a colt in a field on a crisp autumn morning.

Gone were the days of the hot walker and longeing. Hello, track! Albeit, the track at Gary's wasn't but a big dirt oval surrounding a field of grass and encircled by a mountain skyline. Something about the little track against the horizon, though, felt right. From all directions, I was embraced by the bluest, prettiest mountains of all time—blue mountains given their color by the sky surrounding them and the trees covering them.

I liked breezing around and around the track with Filipia so much that when it came time to teach me how to walk into and spring out of a starting gate, I'm proud to say that we had a total of zero serious mishaps.

Sure, I had to be convinced. For that part of my training, Grandfather Dante didn't show up in any of my dreams with any cryptic messages to help me out. I guess he figured that I knew what I needed to do. After a while I got the hang of the gate, and pretty soon, I was loading nicely, breaking well, and beating all the two-year-olds at Gary's. But those weren't really races, were they?

With all of Gary's filming and picture taking, Filipia and I became a sensation in *Kentucky Bloodlines*. Letters from racing fans all the world over started arriving. Everybody wrote in with questions.

When will he run? Where will he run? Will you let the girl race him?

One morning, while I was finishing breakfast and Filipia was tidying up my stall, Gary strolled by. Whistling. Pretty nearly skipping, even.

"Young lady," he said to Filipia. "I'm going to give you an opportunity. I've entered Dante here in a baby race in Charleston next month. You'll take him; no big deal. Can you handle that?"

Now, listen, she was standing in my back blind spot when he said it, but the gleam of that smile of hers liked to knock me down.

"Then, let's get to work," Gary said. "We'll apply for your jockey license when we get there, so get ahold of your birth certificate and whatnot."

For a few blessed weeks, all three of us were in our elements. Gary with his clipboard, recording splits. Filipia in the saddle, singing me songs from her home. And me sailing through workouts like I had been born to float. We never did convince Gary to join us for a swim in the Willis, but he never tired from following us around with that video camera.

Our fans grew. More letters came and carrots and apples and peppermints, too. Those divine morsels never arrived in my bucket, sadly.

A few days before the race, we all three piled in the trailer and headed over to West Virginia. I was about to break my maiden race, and the world was watching.

✳ CHAPTER TWENTY ✳
RACE DAY

Early on race day morning, Filipia slipped into my track stall. All quiet and forlorn. Not bouncing and happy like usual. For once, I greeted her first. I nickered in her ear and nudged her chin.

"Monkey, I'm scared like crazy," she confessed.

Now, in all the days and nights and long, hot afternoons of our training, that girl had never shown a hair of fear. Not a whisker.

Something wasn't right.

She paced around, nervous and suspicious, same way I had acted for most of my life before she showed up to save me.

"Monkey, I have something to tell you. You might be mad at me. What I need to say is . . . well, do you ever feel like you're pretending to be somebody you're not?"

She lowered her head and nuzzled me. Sometimes, I could swear that girl was part horse herself. Now, I had no way to tell her that's exactly how I felt every day. Just thinking about the three tests and worrying whether I'd be good enough got me feeling hemmed up and anxious. I instinctively pulled away from her hold.

"Sorry," she said, and gave me some space. "You're so easy to talk to. Everyone here at the track has a job to do, and they all fit in together. Except for me. I don't belong."

Just then, two jockeys returning from an all-nighter came roaring past us, carrying on about who owed whom what.

The sounds of the backside were by no means harmonic or peaceful.

"See what I mean? Ernesto and Melvin rode against each other yesterday, got drunk together, and couldn't leave each other's sides last night. This morning, they're enemies again but will be friends, again, by sunset. They belong here. I don't."

With his usual awful timing, Gary came stomping around the corner, robbing me of time to reassure Filipia that I would always be her friend and that she did belong. With me.

Gone was the lighthearted Gary who had at least started to cool his bare feet in the river with us. Gone was the Gary whooping and hollering and cheering Filipia and me on during our daily workouts. Vanished, the guy who went all topsy-turvy when he clicked the stopwatch to record my time splits.

Old Sourface was back.

"Chop-chop, Fil. Let's get a move on. Lots to do this morning," he said. "Oh, and here's a temporary license, pending your birth certificate. We've got to get that taken care of. The steward owes me big-time, so you're good to go today. But chop-chop on that, too."

Filipia took a deep breath. Her heartbeat quickened. She stiffened up first in her hands, then her back, and then her jaw. Whatever else was on her mind would have to wait. And I couldn't wait.

Despite all of those fans who had been writing to me, I wasn't winning any popularity contests in Charleston.

"Morning line has us going off at fifty-to-one," Gary told us. But he didn't seem bothered at all. "We like those odds, right? More money. More splash. More to celebrate when you win. That cousin of yours, Covert Agent, is the favorite. You got that?"

Post time came, and we started toward the gate at a medium walk. Filipia's hands gripped my reins tight. Her focus was someplace else, I could tell.

When she asked me to move on to the gate, I picked

up a trot, and then, at last, I felt a big smile break across her face. My partner was back! Whatever had gotten her all worked up earlier had eased along once we were in the dirt.

Just before we reached the start, though, she pulled me up.

"Whoa, Monkey."

I listened to her like always, because we were a team committed to serving and respecting each other. If Filipia needed to stop, well, by goodness, I refused to take another step.

She sighed, then leaned forward to tell me something.

"Look, Dante. Out beyond the track. What do you see?"

I whinnied. Stands of people, the starting gate filling up with horses and jockeys, and an undisturbed oblong track that was making my frogs itchy and my shoes tingly.

"I see the ocean. I see Melon and Mama back home on my island. Melon is waving at me and blowing me kisses. She is telling me to hold my head up and to win. I'm racing for her. Who are you racing for, Monkey?"

I scanned the horizon. Now, I can't say I saw the ocean, but right then as Filipia was using her knowing eye to connect with her family back home on her island, something shifted in my wisdom eye, too. In a dizzy instant, that familiar dense and layered fog came skirting across the field, and the track took on the hue and grade of the rolling green pastures of my Kentucky home. I heard a soft whicker. The fog burned away and a stallion, dark as pitch, like me, stood atop a lush Kentucky hillside. Behind him, all of my grandmothers and grandfathers lifted their heads. I sensed them sending me everything I would need to run. Grandfather Dante stepped forward. A spark passed between us—a charge that must have stretched out across all of time in every direction. That was all I needed.

"Come on," said Filipia, after what felt like an hour but could hardly have been but a few seconds. "The sleeping shrimp gets taken by the current. Let's go!"

Believe me, as hard a time as I gave folks over needles and thermometers and every prick and prod, I pranced right into that starting gate with nary a care.

I looked around for my cousin, Covert Agent, but he wasn't on either side of me. I thought I caught a glimpse of him in a middle gate, but no time to whinny and no time for a family reunion. I had a race to run. The gates were filled up with chestnuts, one or two bays, and me, all black all over.

We posted to the outside. I angled both ears on Filipia. She crouched into position on a saddle weighted to be even with the other horses. She adjusted and readjusted her goggles over her eyes, patted my neck softly, and flashed the whip in her left hand to rev me up.

"Get ready, now, to follow my lead." She cued again with the stick. "All the rain last night has given us a mess. A sloppy river of a track ordered up just for you, Monkey."

I let her situate herself and settle. She picked up the reins, and I welcomed the contact with the bit and her hands.

I relaxed my back. We waited for the gun.

"See the finish, Monkey? Use the knowing eye. Can you see us in the winner's circle?"

And we were off.

We broke the outside. I stumbled, almost to my knees. Filipia lifted my head. I righted myself up and lurched forward.

The crowd cheered.

The field pulled away from us in unison. When the stampede of their hooves started to fade, my face was as clean as a new bucket. We fell well off the pace, not even close enough to eat their dirt.

Filipia drove to the inside, and we quickly closed to ten or so lengths behind the tight pack with no clear leader.

No problem. Hardly a drop of sweat or a labored

breath moved between Filipia and me. I handled the pace with ease.

We held the gap steady. I had hardly exerted to get back in the race, but we had a long way to go yet. Both of us had something to prove. We had come to dominate, not play catch-up.

I wanted to go wild. I begged to cut loose. The track was a muddy mess and it felt good on my feet. We floated; we were in the river, and I wanted to run.

"Not yet, Monkey." Filipia rode high up in the saddle.

I overtook three who were fading. We closed to six lengths behind the leaders. We stalked the field like that for a furlong or two. One by one, horses fell off the pace as Filipia and I started to pick up ours.

Around the last bend, I saw a silky flash to my right, so close I could smell how hard the jockey was working. My jockey still smelled of soap. The petite filly behind me found something more and made a move toward the inside. The sweaty jockey went to the whip. Up front, the leaders pulled half a length ahead. I couldn't wait a whole lot longer. I dug into the bit, begging for the cue to open up.

Finally, Filipia crouched in my ear. "Now, Monkey, go! Go and don't look back."

I took control of the dirt.

We bore down on the five horses in front of us like a tropical storm swinging across the mountains and refusing to dissipate. Filipia brought the sea, and I brought the wind. We found every ready opening, cut in new holes, and raced through each one.

With the finish in sight, Filipia didn't need to ask with the whip. She ducked to the inside, let me run, and we powered down on the leader.

I could see now who was out front! Covert Agent and I were running neck and neck. No matter what, we would finish one and two. Today would be a great day at the track for us, our dams, and Edensway Farm. No matter what, we had done the pedigree proud. The two of us.

But who would it be for the win?

Filipia turned to her right and looked at Covert's jockey, hungover Melvin from the morning.

"Adios, my friend." She tucked low behind me and yelled, "Whatever you have left, Monkey, now is the time. Run like crazy!"

I had at least one gear left. Had the race been any longer, we might have discovered that I had two.

We proved best. A few good people in the stands were very happy, Gary was ecstatic, and that triumph marked the beginning. Although one race does not proof of the bloodlines make, my first race went a long way toward establishing the good name of Dante's Beatrice, Marey, as a broodmare.

Best of all, I loved running with Filipia.

Now that I knew what everything was building toward, I couldn't wait to do it all again.

CHAPTER TWENTY-ONE

BEST LAID PLANS

Covert Agent and I dominated the two-year-old field for the rest of the season. Owned it. Back and forth, we traded the one and two spots, chasing each other around the country. Shoot, I wanted to win every meet, but if I had to lose, then losing to Covert eased the choke. Us winning so much proved a good thing for our dams, for Edensway, and for the pedigree. We showed up, and that's a fact.

What I really needed, though, was one more big win. To seal Marey's future. To set myself up for a life of leisure—grazing bluegrass, perpetuating the bloodlines, and greeting adoring fans. To have a shot at the three tests.

"Give me one more race," Gary said. "Another good win and you'll be a dandy of a three-year-old next spring. You can hold on till then, can't you?"

He selected a good one, all right — Arkansas!

I'd gotten used to and accepting of my routine. Walking onto the trailer meant payday for everybody. Gary and Filipia loaded me up for the big race with plenty of fresh hay on the trailer. I couldn't see the road ahead and couldn't hear Gary and Filipia, who rode up front in the cab. The wind was the only map for me to follow. I liked for the window to stay cracked so I could catch the scents of dew and trees and mountains.

The three of us arrived at the Arkansas track two days ahead of the race in time to get right. By that, I mean get right with the race officials and with the new environment.

Now, as we had seen, some tracks operate more lackadaisically than others. As attached as he was to his clipboard, paperwork was not Gary's strength. There'd be no forgotten paperwork or lost birth certificate in Arkansas. This being our biggest race to date had everybody on edge. Gary's gloomy outlook showed no signs of sunny days ahead. Filipia, all of a sudden, stayed pretty much out of sight. She and Gary were outright arguing, but, for once, not about me.

I was as cool as a mule. Fired up and ready to go. My stall — more like a box, if you ask me — was a bit on the cramped side, but I had a good view of the track and the stands. Horses showed up from all over. Every one of us pretty certain that we'd win this race and get a bid to THE derby in my home state of Kentucky when we turned three. The first of the three great tests.

Of course, my dear cousin, Covert Agent, surfaced in Arkansas, too.

Turns out that with both Covert and me running, the Arkansas race was a big enough deal to draw the entire Eden family into the grandstands. Live and in person on the big day, there came Mrs. Eden, Doctor Tom, and Melody. And Red, right in there with them. They even got themselves a highfalutin viewing box. A real family reunion.

Little Melody didn't seem so small anymore; honestly, I would have recognized her anywhere, because what I most remembered was the way she waved whenever she first spotted me. And her shaggy red mane.

"L.D., look at you, all grown up," Melody said when she came to visit me before post time.

I nickered the same back to her. Oh, sure, Melody stood a might taller. Because the Edens took racing seriously, Melody most certainly did not show up in her barn pants and dirty boots. Behind the flowery hat and lacy gloves, that girl was still Melody.

I reached out toward Melody to search for the scent of Marey or anything familiar. The girl smelled brand spanking new. Not a trace of hay or grain or wet grass on her. No peppermint, either.

Just then Gary came around the corner and tried to shoo her away. "Save the smooching on your colt till after he wins."

"Dante, I have to go back now. You're even odds today, but I'll be cheering for you. Here's a secret. If you win this race, you'll come back to Kentucky. You'll train near home to run for the roses! We're all counting on you."

About the time Melody disappeared from my sight, I heard quite a commotion starting up in the aisle, coming right toward me. One that would sweep me up, whirl me around, and drop me down a hole so far I might never get out.

CHAPTER TWENTY-TWO

SEEING BOTH SIDES

L et me explain, sir, Gary. Wait, please."
I'd never heard Filipia sound so desperate.
Never once detected tears hunkering down in her throat, blocking her voice.

What I had heard aplenty was Gary blowing his top. But his tantrums hadn't been directed at Filipia or me for some time.

Till that meet in Arkansas.

"You're lucky you made it this far without having to prove your age. I'm not going to make a stink about this, nor am I going to tell anybody the real reason why we're changing jockeys. I had a feeling from the get-go. Eighteen, my boots. So how old are you?"

"Sixteen."

Gary stomped his foot, shook his head, and stomped again. "I knew it. I knew it. I knew it."

Filipia stood outside my stall, hanging her head like a filly stuck out in a cold rain with no shelter, no blanket, and no friends. I didn't understand what all had happened, but I sure got the gist.

I nickered and tried to nuzzle her through the bars.

"May I say good-bye to Dante?" she asked Gary.

Whoa, hold it right there, I thought. *Whose idea was good-bye?* I started stomping and kicking up a fuss.

Gary went right on ignoring me. He was angling to get rid of Filipia for good.

"You'd best gather your things. Leave the silks folded in the locker room. I've got a new jockey who'll take Dante today. And we no longer need your services elsewhere."

So he was kicking her to dirt? The direct line between Gary and all that money in his pocket? If I hadn't been contained in a so-called stall that was really a little box about half the size I was used to, I'd have bolted away from the track faster than a storm ripping over the mountains. And I'd have carried my friend Filipia away with me.

I protested and rioted to no avail. Filipia finally gave up, and before she left she tried to tell Gary the secret to what made me run fast.

"Please, at least listen to me about Dante. No way he'll go right unless he can stop and look clear across the field before he goes into the gate. That's important to remember. I don't know what he sees; I just know you can't rush him."

Gary turned to me, then pointed to her. "What do you see right there, Dante? I'll tell you what I see behind those crocodile tears. I see the face of a liar."

Filipia dropped her shoulders and hung her head. True to her word, she did not leave without saying good-bye. "Pumpkin, pumpkin, each and every one to their home. Melon used to tell me that when the fun had been going on for too long. I love you like crazy, Monkey. Thank you." She walked away and didn't look back.

I did some hard thinking about Gary's question. *What does a horse see?*

Two different sides of the same world. Particular to a horse's way of seeing, I expect. These two eyes of mine are situated so that they can take in both sides of a whole.

I think that's a fair piece of what Filipia was trying to explain to Gary. But he wasn't listening to her side.

I suspect she had been trying to tell me all along to enjoy every minute and to learn what I could because she knew it was temporary. I figure she also tried more than once to tell me the truth about her age and about her lie. All that business of pressing her hand between my eyes, instructing me about the so-called knowing place. The true way of seeing.

Maybe, in her own way, Filipia was already trying to explain everything. How she was lying about her age. Maybe she wanted me to know that it wasn't her age that really mattered.

She might have only been sixteen, but in a way, she was older and smarter than all the more experienced horsemen I had met up to that point in my two years of life, including Doctor Tom and Red. Though to be accurate, they were both chestnuts, not grays.

Minutes before post time, there I stood at the Arkansas track waiting to meet a new jockey. Everything that had been right and good and harmonious yesterday was all wrong today. Needless to say, I did not win. Finished dead last. At least Covert won.

* CHAPTER TWENTY-THREE *

TUMBLE DOWN

Naturally, everyone, at first, pinned the Arkansas slide on jockey mismatch. And a mismatch it was, too.

Every last person with an opinion insisted, one way or another, that the real problem was the girl. Some suspected that Filipia had been secretly drugging me. That insulting line of reasoning led exactly nowhere. I tested clean, of course, because I was.

None of the horsemen could fathom why I plummeted so hard and fast the way I did. They looked to the clipboard for theories about my diet, training, rest, intake, and came up with zilch. Hard to believe that nobody—not the Edens, not Gary, nor any of my jockeys—could put up a good answer to the question.

Why can't he run? They wanted to know.

Easy peasy. Filipia spoke the truth when she spoke her parting words, but not a one of them thought to follow her advice. Gary was too stubborn and proud to heed the words of a girl, even though she had told him exactly what to do: give me a few seconds to acclimate and look around before the race. Those few seconds would've made all the difference, but Gary just didn't get it.

Pretty simple stuff. Turns out, she was right. Horses are, well, we're creatures of habit. People count on us equines for that. Heck, I counted on that. A slew of experts around me and not one realized that the habit of pausing to reflect had been started by Filipia and allowed to continue during every race up till Arkansas.

Take that away? Well, what exactly would they expect to happen?

The bottom line: that gathering moment before each race was necessary. Filipia could see it because she's the one who showed me.

I needed a pause before racing in order to follow the knowing place back to the bluegrasses and temperate breeze of Kentucky. Back to where I knew Marey grazed at Edensway. And to where Grandfather Dante had welcomed me into the family on my first day. Real or not, that's just how it was. I needed to walk with the bloodlines before each and every race. They took that away and filled the void with the whip.

For a good piece of the next two seasons, I enjoyed the halo of my winning two-year-old season and, at least initially, didn't bear the burden of the blame for my own downfall. Filipia and I had won some good races and big money back-to-back.

Gary and company kept on sending me right back to the track. He'd been handed the magic to set me up for the win on Filipia's way out the door, and he had promptly and persistently ignored her. Even with so much at stake, old Sourface was too proud, too stubborn, and too sure he could fix me himself to even consider that the girl might have been right.

Every jockey I met after the Arkansas tumble went to the whip early and stayed there. While that tactic does work on some horses, I was not one of them. In true spite of the whip, I won what I needed to win to survive. Just survive.

I had seen enough of what happens to Thoroughbreds who land at the bottom. Though I was but a baby, in many ways, I was wised up enough to the game to know that I needed to run well occasionally to kindle the hope.

As a three-year-old, I raced five times. Gary

himself took me all over. Maryland. West Virginia. Florida. We'd pick up jockeys at whatever track we were running.

Despite Gary's meddling with my blood and oxygen and nerves by dosing me up with any legal substance, and a few that maybe he'd agreed to look the other way on, despite all that fiddle-faddle, I won enough purses to buy my dam and Edensway the time they needed to reestablish their breeding program. Of course, my cousin stayed out there doing his part for Edensway. Covert had sealed his place in the bloodlines. In the meantime, my path was altered.

There are reasons to alter a colt. More reasons to geld than not to, I suppose. Apparent to everyone was that I would never amount to the new-era champion that the racing world pined after. Mrs. Eden decided not to breed me. They had to sedate me to cut me, but cut me they did. Some other colt, maybe Covert, would keep the bloodlines winning.

By then, Marey's next colt, whom I had never met, was two and burning it up. My little half brother. Doctor Tom had bred Marey to a different stallion to clean up the pedigree. My record had at least helped to prove her a good dam.

When I raced as a four-year-old, I remained in the gate for my first three races, never broke. Gary brought me back to Virginia. "We just need to regroup a little bit," he told a reporter from *Kentucky Bloodlines.* "I feel like he's setting on a good race, for sure. I know he can do it. The question is, does he want to?"

As a five-year-old, I raced seven times. Five times I finished dead last. Twice I won. Seems like the older I got the worse I performed.

The funny thing is, in those two races the circumstances of loading into the starting gate did, indeed, give me pause to find the bloodlines, but not a soul recognized the differentiator.

I sure wasn't reeling in a fortune, but winning on ninety-to-one odds, every now and again, kept me barely ahead of even money. Winning enough so that Marey and Edensway Farm would reap some benefits.

Seven different jockeys, a new one for each race. I couldn't tell one from the other. Never knew their names. I'm sure they knew mine.

No doubt, I'd have raced all my life for Filipia.

Almost worked out for both of us.

On reflection, I know the girl lied because she loved me. Shoot, she loved horses. Had lived her entire life among us. And even more so, that child loved her family. Thanks to her, I gave my own family a fair chance at good lives.

Because of the success that Filipia and I had found together, folks were reluctant to give up on me. They knew what I could do. As a result — and I attribute this saving grace to Filipia—nobody sent me to the claiming stakes to run me ragged and empty till my feet and legs and mind were shot. No sir, my jockey's lie was told for my well-being as much as her own.

So, how could I have ever been anything but grateful for Filipia? After Gary fired her, my whole life changed. And my future did, too. Whatever was on my horizon would not include winning Grandfather Dante's Triple Crown. I had tumbled down so far that even a miracle couldn't earn me half a chance at the three tests.

CHAPTER TWENTY-FOUR

FACE THE TRUTH

In a last-ditch effort to salvage something of my career and her investment, Mrs. Eden wielded her influence and got me into a big race in Virginia. Not one reporter from *Kentucky Bloodlines* showed a whiff of interest in the odds or the outcome. We weren't even sure a new jockey could be found to do the job.

One blessed thing about my last race was the same as my first.

Filipia came. And I guess it shocked her how much I had changed.

"Monkey, remember me?"

I whickered softly. *I will never forget.*

She set her hand in between my eyes. I let out a defeated sigh. "Oh, my friend. Are you in there? You look so thin and tired. Like a bag of bones. Where is the fire in your eyes, Monkey?" She walked her fingers along my barrel, counting each of my ribs.

I suppose I finally needed to accept my fate and to acknowledge that, in my case, the bloodlines didn't work out. I wasn't made to be a great racehorse or to face the three great tests. Grandfather Dante had made a mistake.

If Filipia hadn't been there on the day of my last race, I would've dug my hooves deep into the dirt and not budged out of the gate. Taken the whip, for the whip was surely coming my way, start or no start.

But I wanted to run for Filipia. Just before we entered the gate, I saw her in the stands, and we locked gazes. For Filipia, I gave it my all and finished in the middle of the pack. Nothing to be proud of, but no shame, either.

After the race, she came to tell me good-bye. "Dante," she said, "you're on the verge of a breakdown. I promise you will not race again. If I have anything to do with anything, you're done."

Just then Mrs. Eden came around the corner with Gary. The two of them locked in a whisper. You'd best believe neither of them was happy to see the girl who was really to blame. According to them, anyway.

Filipia pleaded my case. Neither Gary nor Mrs. Eden wanted to hear what she had to say. Nor did they want to face the truth. I had been worked to the ground, chasing for fortune.

"I'll make a call," Mrs. Eden said. "No promises."

And so ended my career as a racehorse. The pedigree needed champions to win and stallions to breed. I was neither.

CHAPTER TWENTY-FIVE

STRAIGHT OFF THE TRACK

The bloodlines granted me two last favors that day at the track. First, Filipia had showed up. She was still living in Virginia and had read I'd be racing. Second, she had succeeded in persuading Mrs. Eden to call up a nearby Thoroughbred retirement program. They had room to spare and were already on their way to the track for two fillies.

Though it was tempting to get down in the jowls about being all used up at age five, I knew life could have turned down a much harder road.

Why, just that very evening along the backside they'd had to put down the winner of the state derby. She was a horse in the wrong place at the wrong time.

She'd hardly cooled down from her race when the fire-works finale went up and scared the lights out of that big bay filly. She reared, and it was a grotesque sight to witness her strike a pole with her head, then twist and turn and injure herself to the point of no return. Life quickly drained out of her, and though her trainer eased her suffering in the final moments, her ending was a sad and sorry shame. They say she was on her way to becoming a true champion. A gal that could run with the boys. A tragic ending, for sure. God love that filly. Her racing career ended that day, and her life did, too.

Somehow, though, I'd been spared. I had been blessed early and often, showed my backside to destiny, yet the second chance shifted my way because Filipia loved me.

We had very little time for good-byes. Mrs. Eden and Gary were visibly relieved to let me go.

With tears in her eyes, Filipia walked me to the trailer. "Melon always says that God's greatest act was to make one day follow another. Tomorrow is a new day, Monkey."

Straight from the track in Virginia, three of us worn-down racehorses rode away together. The other two passengers, both fillies, were at least a hand smaller than I was and quieter, too. The bay one resembled Marey. The red was all red and not a spot of white. She took after Covert.

Neither filly touched their hay. Not a bite. They couldn't hardly lift their heads to look out the window, much less pull hay. There wasn't much to see out on the road, anyway. Not a mountain in sight. Nor a hill that could make me think of home.

As we didn't have a terrible far distance to travel, I got to smelling their hay, and it seemed a shame to let it all go stale, especially since both the fillies' nets were within my easy reach.

Neither one put up a lick of fuss at sharing. That's how I knew they were in a world of hurt. I could only hope that the place we were headed would look kindly upon all three of us.

Long about dusk, the trailer stopped, and we unloaded. I was downright stunned to find that the entire farm was enclosed by a tall barbed-wire fence. Nobody would be breaking out of there.

The handlers led us to a brick barn with cement floors. Our hooves struck the ground in alternating beats and set off a welcoming chain of whinnies and nickers down the lane. There must have been twenty Thoroughbreds, all former racers, already living in that big barn.

They led me to a stall at the very end on the corner, next to a chestnut about my size who had his nose to the wall and his rear toward the door. The bay filly was placed across the aisle. She was even dimmer in the eyes than at the start of our trip. As soon as she took her first couple of steps, I could see that she was off. Lame.

The night men tossed a flake of hay in each of our stalls and filled up two buckets each with water. "Welcome to Riverside Maximum Security Correctional Center," said the man leading me. "Also known as prison."

CHAPTER TWENTY-SIX

PRISON

In the daylight, the new place was full of horses and men. The men they called offenders all wore the same type of denim britches, and they worked under the watchful eyes of other men called guards, who carried guns, so I tried hard to be good.

We retirees in the program had seen everything there was to see. Seen glory and agony. On the track, when a horse broke down a stride or two ahead of you, what choice was there but to go over, under, or around. I'd seen a whole lot worse, too. Things no man or horse should ever have to see.

And yet, there I was. Standing on four feet. Breathing in fresh air and trying to fathom finding a second chance and wondering what on earth I might do with my remaining years if not race. And wondering if I could ever learn to do anything else.

I saw plainly that Mrs. Eden had sent me to retire on a Virginia prison farm where, it seemed to me, fallen horses and fallen men landed with a thud. Everybody inside needed some kind of fixing or correcting or rehabilitating. Somewhere along the way, somebody had gotten the idea that we could help one another.

The purpose of bringing second-chance hopefuls like myself into the prison environment was to test out this idea that, maybe somehow, broken men could help broken horses, and vice versa. Take my situation. Pretty simple. I needed a place to live and someone to care for me. The men confined to the prison farm had time to learn and time to give.

Now, the main elements of the retirement program included (1) make a good match between a man and a Thoroughbred, (2) teach the man how to care for and understand horses, and (3) help the ex-racehorse just be a horse. I didn't reckon the fourth goal would ever apply to me: adopt out the ex-racehorses into forever homes, where we could live out the last, oh, twenty-five or so years of our lives.

The success of this whole experiment turned on the idea that friendship and structure would put the horses and the men back together. Rebuild confidence and make us whole again.

Right away, I started learning and unlearning. The woman in charge, Miss Bet, said the main thing I needed to figure out was how to be a horse. She recommended that after all I'd been through, what I deserved was time off my toes, grazing in the sunshine. Experiencing what it felt like to nuzzle and nicker and stand and graze.

Don't know that I deserved anything but what I had gotten, especially for not holding up my end of the bargain and being unable to keep my promise to Marey. My siblings were out there winning, doing their part, and, I supposed, Grandfather Dante was helping them along, the way he had tried to help me.

About every week somebody or another would come visit the prison program, shopping for a horse with good bloodlines to adopt. Folks came by seeking a mare that might make a fine hunter or even emerge into a good jumper. Other visitors were in the market for a Thoroughbred to make their pasture look more beautiful. I turned a few heads, but nobody called me in from the paddock.

Miss Bet had some preplanned messages that she liked to deliver to potential new owners. I liked listening to her lay down the law of the off-the-track Thoroughbred like only Miss Bet could do.

"I don't need to tell you that these horses are

highly specialized. Everything in their breeding, their upbringing, and their training is oriented to a life on the track. I know we're at the dawn of the Thoroughbred revolution, but you can't expect to throw a saddle on an OTTB and put them to work. That's a risky venture for all involved, especially the horse." She'd often start with something along those lines.

"I know," visitors would typically say. "I'm ready for a more advanced horse."

"Is that right? Stall number twenty literally bit off Ralph's thumb last Friday. Well, almost took it off. He doesn't like pitchforks. Care to imagine why?"

"Oh, I can imagine. That's why I'm here."

Then, if her guest flashed a glance toward me, and they often did, because what can I say, people like black horses, she'd warn them off. "You noticed the black gelding behind you? He'd as soon kick your ankles from under your knees as wait for you to set his grain bucket down."

Oh, I knew my future read bleak as far as any hope for getting adopted from the program.

Now, Miss Bet and some nice volunteers from the community trained the men to work at a high level directly with us track retirees. Every horse had a man assigned, and they all received training, but something about my propensity to kick, charge, and threaten made Miss Bet think I needed a different type of handler.

Lucky for me, such a man had made his own mistakes and landed himself at Riverside and right outside my stall door.

First time I met John the Farrier, he stood at my door just staring at me. Not talking up a blue streak. Not holding a feed bucket. Looking directly at me.

I found his overall demeanor on the threatening side. Lucky for him, he kept on his side of the stall door. Had he stepped into my personal space, staring me down as he was, my snaking head would have only been the start of his troubles.

I figured I'd best send a clear and swift signal to this fellow so if he ever did get a mind to enter my space, he'd think twice. I wasted no time. I spun on my haunches and kicked the holy Hades out of the door, with him standing right there. *Bam-bam-bam.* I just slammed my two back hooves up against that door till it rattled. Then I reloaded and fired off another quick round. John the Farrier jumped back like a grasshopper.

Enough said, I figured, so I gave him my backside and enjoyed myself some hay. Hardly any ways into my peace, here he came back again. Looking directly at me, again.

What he did next surprised the fierce right out of me. John cleared his throat and started up with a song. Crooning at the top of his lungs to me about walking on through wind and rain and all sorts of trouble.

His voice was terrible. In a sort of involuntary protest, my back leg raised up to kick out whenever his notes went sharp. Creaking and cracking and pitching up and down, he sang on. Loud. Sure. And right to me.

Every time his voice wavered I could feel the struggle in him. A kind of inside suffering that was familiar to me. The determined lyrics and his melancholy tone spoke to my heart. Maybe even woke up a part of my heart that I had stomped down. I recognized in John some of the same voices that lived deep in me.

Not good enough.

Not wanted.

A failure and a disappointment.

I recognized something else, too. There was a big difference between that broken man and this broken horse. John the Farrier was trying. I had already given up.

I nodded my head and, awful as those rancid notes sounded, I hoped he'd keep singing, because John revealing himself to me and not caring if he was perfect or even good enough sounded like an invitation and a promise. When he finished, the two of us stood still. Watching each other. I curled my nostrils toward him. Sure enough, from somewhere on his person wafted the aroma of peppermint.

I nickered.

"May I come in now?" he asked me.

I prided myself on having cultivated the habit

of showing respect when it was first shown me, so I stepped back, and so began our good partnership.

Before he found trouble, John had worked around the region as a farrier, shoeing and trimming ponies and horses. In addition to working on our feet, one of his main jobs inside the prison was to reeducate us about being under saddle.

In racing, I had used one gait predominantly: fast. With a pocket full of peppermints and a repertoire packed with praise, John managed to get me tacked up and himself perched in the saddle. I had my reservations about John. Being a good farrier does not a good rider make, necessarily. John could ride about as well as he could sing. The tension in his jaw let on that he had some reservations about me, too.

Miss Bet had tried to warn him. "He'll have better focus if you longe him before work. To help him soften up," she said, but he ignored her advice.

I tried to oblige him, but every time I'd pick up the pace, he'd lose his balance, pitch forward on my neck, and then pull back tight in my mouth.

He cooed soft sounds, trying to fend off impending disaster, which I believe he knew was coming. "Good boy, good boy. That's it. Relax," John said.

But when he pressed his bony ankle into my side, I bucked him right off. I've never liked pointy things. Not needles. Not ankles.

CHAPTER TWENTY-SEVEN

CHIN UP

A whole year passed. Different Thoroughbreds arrived and others found homes. Some became jumpers. Some learned to hunt. One old gentleman adopted four OTTBs merely to decorate his hills.

John and I worked every day, helping each other toss out old habits and build up new ones. Much as I loved my friend the farrier, I knew that one day he would earn his way free, and I would be left at Riverside without him.

Until then, with nothing but time on his hands, John set himself to learning how to ride. Miss Bet instructed us almost every day. She also encouraged John to spend as much time with me on the ground as in the saddle.

"Try this," Miss Bet suggested. "Get out in the field with Dante. Experiment in his world. Stand beside him as he grazes and do what he does. When he steps forward, you step with him. If he picks up his left foot, you pick up yours. Pretty soon you'll start to feel his center of gravity shift. Awareness, John. Of your body and his. Of your mind and his."

The farrier was a good student and did exactly as he was told. One day he waltzed into my pasture without a halter and without a single peppermint in his pocket that I could detect. I had come to expect my candy, no getting around that fact. At first, when I didn't get what I wanted, I stomped my foot. Then I gave John a knock in the shoulder with my head.

"Buddy, I'm empty-handed today. All I've got is the gift of time and friendship. If you stop acting so spoiled, maybe a story or a song."

He reached his hand up to pet my muzzle, and my lips tickled his fingers, still searching for something sweet that was not there. I was about to get real fussy with him when he lightly scratched between my ears at the top of my poll. The place I had the dangedest time reaching myself. At that instant, my overwhelming desire for peppermint surrendered to the good feeling of standing beside my friend in the broad sunshine, listening to him tell me about his family and his mistakes.

"I guess I'm more like you than I thought, Dante.

My whole life I've lived at two speeds: fast and faster. The fact that I can now walk you around in circles without getting bored or bouncing off the sky, that's a miracle. I'm talking about a miracle in me, not you. When my mama came to visit me last week, know what she said?"

I sure did want to hear that, and John was going to tell me either way, so I just nodded and kept right on grazing and flicking the flies away with my tail. I let him tell his story at his own pace.

"She told me I looked good and sounded better, calmer, and smarter than I had in all my life. 'Prison agrees with you, son.'"

He laughed and shook his head. "I said, 'Nah, Mama, working with that black Thoroughbred agrees with me. Seeing him try so darn hard to change his ways makes me try, too. Watching him start to trust me has changed my whole world.' That's what I told her, buddy."

On such bright days, a sense of hope managed to survive in me, but sometimes, when it was cold or gray outside, a cloudy regret hunkered down over me, for no one had shown any real interest in giving me a forever home. It was that kind of a day when John came to the barn, all dressed up, clean smelling, and with his hair fixed up and no dirt under his fingernails. The only thing about him that smelled right was the peppermint in his pants pocket.

"Hey, buddy," he said, and offered me the candy.

John very likely didn't even realize how he made a habit of delivering bad news with his next two words.

"Sorry, boy," he said. "I'm leaving today. One thing's for sure. I'll miss ya. I can't thank you enough for all you done for me. You might not even know the whole of it." He squinted his eyes even though the sun was hiding behind those dense, smoky clouds. "Never in a million years would I have thought that a horse would help me quit and start and be a better man. But you did. And I thank you."

Naturally, a part of me wanted to pen him to the wall and keep him there. But I knew the deal. Prison wasn't supposed to be a forever home for John. Not for me, either. Riverside was intended to be a place where, if we worked on all those parts of us that needed quitting and starting, if we opened our hearts to new possibilities, both of us might possibly get a second chance. If John was leaving for his, well, good for him.

"Chin up, boy. I'll be around a few more hours. This isn't our last good-bye. Miss Bet wants to interview me and close out my file."

As it happened, on the very day of John's graduation from the school of second chances, a Mrs. Isbell Maiden, from outside of Lexington, Virginia, not Kentucky, visited the retirement program with one of her students, a girl named Ashley.

"Always good to see you, Isbell." Miss Bet extended her hand to the tall, slender woman. "A little surprised, though. You've come an awfully long way and, maybe, to the wrong place if you're looking for a school horse."

"Not exactly. Looking for more of a project horse that we can work with over time."

Everybody that came there wanted a project horse, it seemed to me.

"I've got twenty projects for you to choose from. Anybody catch your eye on the way in?"

Miss Bet enlisted John to stick around and help show them three chestnuts—two geldings and a mare. I had raced and beat each of them. Pummeled the geldings. The mare gave me a chase, though. Now, here these three redheads were beating me to another chance.

Not a one of us would be racing again, that's for sure. Oh, no. In fact, we were all busy undoing everything that we had paid so dearly to learn.

My knees were as straight as the wood planks in my stall. They'd been broken, scraped, and reset to perfection. I had one letter and five numbers tattooed to the inside of my upper lip. Tail to withers, my spine liked to hurt all day and all night. And for what?

For the opportunity to ride around in circles? To be some lady's project? No, thank you.

Outside, the chestnut with a blaze down the front of

his face and withers that sloped like mountains entered the round pen with Miss Bet. I turned one ear toward him. Whenever Miss Bet said "whoa," he twitched his ears to show her he was listening, and he stopped on a dime.

He's a good horse, I thought. *Someone will want him.*

Tacking up that guy didn't require the same rigmarole as it did for me. When I raised my head again, the girl was in the saddle.

"Try a sitting trot," Mrs. Maiden called out. The girl bumped along, and the chestnut never broke his stride.

She asked if she could try the chestnut at the canter. I don't know if the two women saw him flinch, but I sure did. A little tremor ran the length of the red gelding's back. Hesitation is its own sort of warning.

"You know what? That's okay, Bet," Mrs. Maiden said. "Don't worry about it. We don't need to see him canter today." So she had noticed his engine switch on when he heard the word *canter.* One thing's for sure, OTTBs like speed. We're bred for nothing but.

Ashley dismounted, and as good as he was at attempting to ignore the itch to keep moving, the chestnut started prancing to the side before the girl could touch her feet to the ground. Miss Bet and Mrs. Maiden had to hold him for her to safely dismount.

"He's nice," Ashley said, smiling. "I like him."

They walked back through the barn, and Miss Bet turned up the sales pitch. She reeled off his statistics: wins, starts, and, of course, dollars.

I didn't figure I had even earned a look, though my raven coat was showing signs of returning to its former gleam and my weight felt about right. The horse under discussion was not as flashy as I was, but he was better mannered. I lowered my head to find my hay, regretful I had let myself even get interested in this lady and her student.

While Miss Bet and Mrs. Maiden talked, Ashley, who appeared bright and bouncy like Filipia but younger, skipped down the aisle, visiting with each horse. Watching Ashley address each of us with such affection, and observing each horse try so hard, made me happy. For some reason, the old competitive spirit rose up. My ears stood at attention and my heart beat double time. Shoot, I wanted every fine one of us to make a good home. I surely did, but for some reason, I had taken a shine to the girl right away.

My stall was last on the row, and I estimated she'd never reach me. She cooed and kissed at each orphaned horse and read their names and their winnings from the plaques outside the stall doors. 'Course it's not like the size of our purses mattered a whole heck of a lot anymore, but big winnings never failed to impress. That's about the only way any of us really had of showing that we had ever been worth anything.

Some of the horses tried to nuzzle her through the bars. Others turned away and put their noses in the corner. Even though I was last on the end, I listened and waited.

"Look how long your ears are," she said to the dark bay mare.

"Mrs. Maiden, this one has dainty little feet," she said. "So small and sweet." The brown gelding nickered.

Finally, she did approach my stall, but one of the guards warned her from coming any closer.

"Look but don't touch," he said. "Dante's not ready for adoption. Might not ever be." I saw him circle his finger around and around his temple. "Head case."

The woman, Mrs. Maiden, looked alarmed when she heard that. "Ashley, come back over here by me."

Everyone has a label, and, I suppose, I don't really like labels. To me, a man is a man until he is a monster. And a horse is a horse until he's not.

The girl looked back over her shoulder at me, but I turned away.

CHAPTER TWENTY-EIGHT

A Chance

D ante?" Ashley broke away from her trainer and ignored the previous warning.

My eye met Ashley's. A sure look of recognition came over her face as she read my nameplate.

"Dante's Inferno. I thought so!"

Ashley tilted her head like she already knew me. I had the sensation of wanting to know her, too. The black curly hair and thick eyebrows and dark, lively eyes with a sparkle in them made me recall Filipia.

Ashley ran back to where John, Miss Bet, and Mrs. Maiden were standing, across the aisle. He's a grandson of Dante's Paradiso, right?" Miss Bet nodded. "When I was little, I watched him race on TV," Ashley said.

"Did he win?" Mrs. Maiden asked.

"No, he came in last. But, see, he had a new jockey who didn't understand him."

"What makes you say that?"

"Because I watched him. I could tell that Dante wanted to stop and look at the track and all the horses, but his jockey whipped him to make him go on. Then Dante started bucking and rearing. He was so lathered by the time they got him to the gate, he didn't have anything left. I felt sorry for him. I just have always thought that if they had only let him look around until he was ready . . . he would have won."

"He sounds like a bit of a handful!" Mrs. Maiden said.

"But couldn't we give him another chance? You've been saying that we need a fancy horse who could make it all the way to the A-shows someday."

"I thought you liked the chestnut."

"I do, a lot. But everybody has a chestnut. Dante is all black. He's so gorgeous. I just know he'll be great."

Mrs. Maiden returned to give me a closer look. At first, I backed up into the corner and pawed the ground, but then Mrs. Maiden spoke softly, like she meant no harm.

Miss Bet helped me out. "He's skittish. Not very

trusting, at first. I hate to imagine why. But watch this."
Miss Bet unwrapped a peppermint—she always kept
one or two in her pocket. Just a whiff soothed me.

"See how daintily he takes the candy?"

Ashley pressed her face to my stall. I lifted my nose
to hers. "Oh, Dante! You can learn to be a riding horse,
can't you? A hunter or, maybe, one day a jumper? And
we have trails, too! Well, Mrs. Maiden does. She's my
teacher."

Despite myself, truly, I nickered. That took Miss
Bet by surprise and made John laugh. The girl giggled,
which made me nicker again. And before I knew it,
Ashley was standing in my stall, pressing her nose to
mine asking was I happy. Then offering to trade breaths
with me.

"Let me scratch your ears," she said in the
kindest way.

"He loves that," John said. "You might just make a
new friend if you keep it up."

When I didn't drop my head straightaway, Ashley
peered down into me and revived the one single human
word that all at once could make me happy and sad and
assured and relaxed.

"Monkey," she said, "you're twitching your ears
like crazy. Everything's okay." She combed her fingers
through my forelock. "That's what my mom always
calls me, only she's away right now."

Ashley called me Monkey. I dropped my head and leaned into her hands.

"That's a good sign," Mrs. Maiden said.

"Like I said, the issue with Dante is trust. With time, he could be incredible. I'll be honest. He's a big question mark, but he is a gorgeous mover, for sure. If you have the time, I'd love to show him to you."

Though I'm sure he was ready to leave prison behind, my good friend John didn't let me down. Despite him being all cleaned up and dressed in street attire, he didn't hesitate when Miss Bet pressed him into service one last time. He tacked me up and led me out to the small riding ring, then longed me first, as had become our routine and part of his cue for me to settle down.

I snagged a peppermint from him, too, so that counted as a good day.

With Mrs. Maiden and Ashley looking on, I devoted attention to John, adjusting my ears toward his voice, so that everybody would see how they were watching a talented horse.

"I started with Dante about a year ago," said John. "He's still got a lot to learn, but he's a good thinker. Very willing and a heart of gold, once you get down in there and find it. He needs work every day, but if you've got the time to invest, there's no limit to his abilities. He'll be outstanding. Eventually."

"I see what you mean. His ground manners leave something to be desired, but the horse *is* a nice mover," said Mrs. Maiden. "Bet, could Ashley try him?"

"What do you think, John?" Miss Bet asked my friend.

John must've had a good feeling about the match being made right there in his last few hours with me. "He's focused and warmed up now. Should be fine."

So John dismounted, and Ashley strapped on her helmet and stepped onto the mounting block, then sat in the saddle.

"Maybe just an easy walk to get a feel for him," Mrs. Maiden suggested.

Ashley was holding her breath, and her whole little body felt tense and wound up, as mine often did before I'd had a minute to collect myself.

"I can tell he wants to go," Ashley said. "I have no leg on him at all and he just wants to move. I can feel it."

"Well, he likes you. That's obvious," said Miss Bet. "John got bucked off on his first ride."

Ashley laughed nervously. "What would he be doing if he didn't like me?"

"Tossing his head. Trying to jerk the reins out of your hands." Miss Bet turned to Mrs. Maiden. "I won't lie to you. He's *very* green, Isbell. He needs a lot of work. Years even."

Ashley let out a big sigh, then so did I. She loosened

her tight grip on the reins, relaxed into her seat, and sighed again. When she started singing under her breath, I lowered my head and just enjoyed the moment. I had learned first from Filipia and then from John that a singing or storytelling rider is someone trying to find their courage and hoping to be my friend. Ashley stayed in the saddle just long enough for me to decide that being friends with her was something I'd like to try.

Somewhere between the first and second peppermint, I had convinced myself that Mrs. Maiden and Ashley would adopt me, but they got in their empty trailer and left the prison with me standing there, wondering how I could have persuaded them to try. Just try me.

Mrs. Maiden had promised to call Miss Bet if they changed their minds, but bereft and forlorn, I couldn't figure out what I had done wrong.

I had been on my best behavior. No stomping. No tail flashing and no rearing. For the first time in a long time, since my winning days with Filipia, I actually wanted something.

I gathered from the talk around me that Mrs. Maiden liked me, all right, and Ashley adored me. But Mrs. Maiden wanted a horse that could help her attract new students to the Maury River Stables and help students such as Ashley progress in their riding. I was too green. Too much of a project horse.

On his way out the door for good, John himself delivered the bad news. "Sorry, boy," he said. "I'm proud of you. You were a good horse today. Shoot, you are every day. I'm not one to wish away my life or throw away my freedom, but I almost wish I weren't leaving here, because of you."

In gratitude for all he'd done for me, I lifted up my right leg, held it high in the air, and made a little pawing action. My way of telling him to come in closer. What's so great about John is that he got me from the get-go.

He laughed. "You're about the best horse. You take some getting used to. Kind of like scotch, but not as bad for me." He rubbed my mane and spoke into my ear. "I love ya, Dante. I hope we meet again."

CHAPTER TWENTY-NINE

COME BACK

Truly, I don't expect a single living soul in the paddock or the barn to believe me, but here's the truth. Some few minutes after John left, I was still grieving over him being gone and still questioning what had happened with Mrs. Maiden and Ashley. I was just about to really give in to feeling sorry for myself, when what did I see but the Maury River Stables trailer come driving past the guardhouse, through the prison gate, and down the hill to the OTTB barn. The two of them pulled right back into the drive of my barn, and that's a fact.

I had pictured the both of them in my mind's eye, and here they came back. Now, such a practice doesn't always work. I am all the time picturing more grain or a few peppermints without producing the desired results.

But this time, visualizing worked. I had been standing on the hill near the road behind the high barbed-wire fence, taking inventory of all the opportunities I'd been given in my life. Some I had taken and others I had not.

Now, I know that not everybody likes their horses poetic and philosophical. Well, blame the bloodlines. If the whole line of us is named after a poet, you can expect we might wax poetic now and again.

I won't lie and say that I ever missed Doctor Tom, Gary, or most of my jockeys. But there are a few folks I've met who really do believe what I believe. Simple as this: we're all animals. Or maybe, we're all commodities. At any rate, we're all in this together.

I hesitate to say equal. That'd cause a controversy in equine and human circles, both species being highly convinced that they're God's own gift.

Few and far between were the humans I had met up to that point who would look me in the eye and swap the truth.

Melody. Filipia. John.

That's it.

All three of them gone. Moved on.

That had got me to thinking about Mrs. Maiden and Ashley. Their visit tapped my heart in the same easy place. Ashley and I had connected. Or so I had thought, until she and Mrs. Maiden left. Without me.

Now here they were, coming around the bend right at the very instant that I had imagined them.

Had they left something valuable behind? What in the world could they want?

CHAPTER THIRTY

A River and a Mountain

Aside from Mrs. Maiden wanting to support her friend Miss Bet's OTTB program at Riverside, I couldn't guess what made her turn that trailer around. But I heard her say to Miss Bet, "It's not every day you meet a horse with a pedigree like Dante's," and she adopted me and transported me to the Maury River Stables that afternoon. By suppertime, I was elated to find myself back in the blue mountains that reminded me of Filipia. Though not the same as my Kentucky home, the blue mountains were a good next best.

The order of things at the Maury River Stables was pretty easy to figure out. Mrs. Maiden had put together a good-working setup for a family riding school: an outdoor ring as you entered the compound, a round pen for new arrivals or hot horses like me who needed longeing like they needed air. A big barn with stalls down both sides, with a small area for riding indoors when the weather was cold or wet or hot. Nothing fancy about the place. A wash stall, a feed room, a tack room, an office, and cross-ties for shoeing. That's it.

Well, not entirely. There was one thing on the outside of the barn that surprised me. A ramp. I confess, prior to my arrival at the Maury River Stables, I held the incorrect opinion that a human being must be able to walk in order to lead a horse. The facts before me required me to rethink that notion, and here's what I learned. Legs don't lead; intention leads. Confidence and energy, too. That ramp outside the barn was built for the express purpose of giving riders who are mobile with the aid of a wheeled chair access to the saddle.

I've now seen this with my own eyes, many a time, and I am no longer amazed, as I was early on. Not that anybody has ever invited me to participate in this type of riding, which is called therapeutic, by the way.

Not all riders in the therapeutic riding school use the ramp. Fact is, I know of blind horses, like the old App here now, and blind riders. No lie. And even though I am not a therapeutic teacher, I've learned a thing or two from the students and horses in the program.

Well, I'm getting ahead of myself again. Back to the setup at Mrs. Maiden's place.

I discovered that she kept two front fields near the barn—one for mares and one for geldings—and a couple more around back. Mrs. Maiden used these primarily for separating us. And she maintained trails leading every which way. Up, down, and all around through the forest, past the pond, across the Maury River, and to the top of Saddle Mountain.

Of everything about my new home, I was most grateful for that river and that mountain. Being a horse who had until then spent his whole life going fast—trying to be first, or fighting life every step of the way—I expect I needed the quenching of the river and the grounding of the mountain as much as I had ever needed anything in my life.

But even with a good river and a strong mountain, being the new horse was lonely.

I met a real mishmash of horses my first day at the Maury River Stables and not a Thoroughbred among them. None of them was too impressed with my bloodlines, and not a one of them even had a pedigree to speak of. I had my pedigree, all right, but not one friend. Shoot, as long as I had grain, hay, and Ashley, why would I need friends anyway?

✶ CHAPTER THIRTY-ONE ✶

FOREVER AND A DAY

After completing the requisite one week with turnout only in the round pen—Mrs. Maiden's attempt to quarantine off any bad germs a new horse might introduce to the barn—I settled in the gelding field. My new home was a ten-acre pasture full of boarded horses with common, untraceable names: Cowboy, Jake, Charlie. And one decidedly uncommon little fella. A purebred Shetland named Napoleon.

Of all those I had met at my new home, Napoleon fascinated me most of all. He was the smallest horse I had ever met and, in a way, the biggest. He used his size to his every advantage, especially when it came to getting out of tricky places. And his confidence was, well, let's just agree that his ego was mountain-size, not miniature. What I liked about the Shetland was that he called me "Mister Dante" from the get-go. A respectful little pony, for sure.

But the very instant I turned out with those other geldings, I met trouble. At Gary's, I never spent much time with horses, nor did I at Riverside. Not in the same field, anyway. Mostly I was kept in a small paddock by myself.

Here, the boarders crowded around me, sniffing my flank and generally being bothersome. Blocking my way. Whinnying right up in my face.

Did I care to have them that close and all up in my business? No, I did not. They cramped my space and wouldn't relent, so I pinned my ears back. That message was clearly received by not a one of them. The boarders kept on bothering me till I had a decision to make, and I decided to throw a conniption fit of squealing, kicking, and, I'm not ashamed, even growling.

I'll be honest. My relations with the other geldings went from sorry to downright catastrophic.

The boarders kept on with their constant picking at me and racing around and around, taunting me about my pedigree, and speculating that I must not be very fast if I was grazing in a field at the foot of Saddle

Mountain. Got me so overloaded with stress that I will freely admit to going on the offensive. If Cowboy even looked my way, I'd flash my teeth. Jake really crossed my line when he violated the invisible circle of my personal space while I tried to graze. No lie, I left a furious hoofprint on his haunch that is somewhat visible to this very day.

You'd think Charlie might have learned his lesson from observing his compatriots, but no. He had to go and show everybody all about being a daredevil. He snatched some hay right out from under me, and I bit the fool right out of his neck. Nah, I take that back. Wiping the fool off Charlie is one impossible thing, for sure.

Here's the surprise. Mrs. Maiden cut me no slack. None at all. In her estimation, the problem resided with one horse and one horse only. Yours truly, Dante's Inferno.

"Dante doesn't know how to befriend horses," she explained to her students. "He only knows how to compete with them."

Maybe she was right, too. I resented the riffraff, and they me. I was fast learning that living in a herd of horses of all sizes and breeds was about as difficult an endeavor as I had ever attempted.

At that point in time, I wasn't in training for anything. My main job was to eat grass, Mrs. Maiden having been advised by the Thoroughbred retirement program that some benefit might be gained from letting me stand around in a pasture for another few months. Even though John had been training me in the basic aids at Riverside, the conventional wisdom said that what I needed most was to work on my ground manners and get accustomed to my new life as a regular-old, nothing-special horse.

If the geldings presented a challenge for me, well, so did the people. Not including Ashley, Mrs. Maiden's students complained, up and down, right and left, that I bullied and bossed every horse and human who stepped into the field.

I didn't see my actions early on exactly as bullying. When a horse has a known and understandable fear of sharp edges, pokers, pointers, sticks, and the like, it seems downright foolish, if not mean, to enter his stall with a pitchfork in your hand, angled directly at him.

Yes, such a travesty happened once, maybe twice, and, yes, I reared up, showed my whites, and stomped a fierce beat until the little pitchfork-carrying culprit left me alone. And that turned into me scaring Mrs. Maiden's students? An injustice.

My saving grace was Ashley. She came out to visit every day. During her school week, we'd have an hour or two of dwindling daylight. On the days without school, she'd spend the sun with me.

I can honestly say I had never met a soul as kind to me as Ashley. Not to take a thing away from Filipia. My jockey was as good as grain, on all occasions, but she had a bit of a temper and was predisposed toward getting frustrated with herself. And when that little gal got annoyed with Gary, she could kick a wall with the best of them. More than once, we kicked the tarnation out of a wall together.

At the Maury River Stables, nobody else seemed all that interested in kicking walls, but what other means of communication did I have for letting Mrs. Maiden know when grain was running late, the hay tasted dry, or my bedding needed changing?

Saddle Mountain knows how I tested Ashley with my bad habits, and kicking was the least bothersome. When I'd spook and bolt away from her or screech to a halt, Ashley never broke toward me in anger. I even thought things were going well until I overheard Mrs. Maiden tell Ashley otherwise.

"I have never given up on a horse before, but if Dante can't start to get along with the other horses and learn to behave no matter who handles him, I'll have no choice but to surrender him back to Riverside."

Ashley dropped her head. "I was hoping we might try to get him ready for the first summer show at Tamworth Springs."

Mrs. Maiden put her hands on her hips. Her voice

went up way high. "You're not even riding him yet, Ashley. Way too early to even think of showing him. Any student of mine ought to be able to muck the stall of any horse in this barn without feeling scared while they're in there. Talk to me about showing him when you can easily pick his feet, safely get him tacked up, and quietly lead him to the ring."

Ashley pleaded with me to try harder. "Can you even understand me? I promise to help you, but you have to want to change, too. The other kids are scared of you. Napoleon's the only horse who likes you. I love you, too, but that's not enough."

The question of the day proved not to be can a racehorse change, but could *this* racehorse change?

Well, maybe. If you've got forever and a day, but I didn't have that kind of time.

CHAPTER THIRTY-TWO

SHADOWS AND LIGHT

I needed some help and fast. An expert. A mentor. That kind of horse wasn't grazing in my field. Sure, Napoleon had a strong résumé of experience with Mrs. Maiden and the Maury River Stables, but he didn't have the look of eagles. By that, I mean the Shetland was most concerned with the moment in front of him and the hay at his feet. I needed to find an equine with a longer, deeper perspective. One who understood what it meant to look out along the distant mountains and tap into the wisdom of the bloodlines and knowingness of the ages. A horse like me.

Alongside the western edge of my field was the mare field, which shared a fence line with the geldings.

Mostly boarded horses lived there, the exceptions being two school horses belonging to Mrs. Maiden: Gwen and Daisy.

Anybody could see that Gwen, a blood bay Hanoverian with three white socks, had a strong maternal instinct toward every horse and every rider. I wondered if she might not be growing tired of keeping things in order. Little fights over hay and water tended to break out regularly among the mares. Though quite regal in appearance, Gwen seemed more interested in teaching and mentoring than enforcing a strong rule of order.

Whereas Gwen's second in command, a little old flea-bitten gray Welsh cob named Daisy who stood at least two hands smaller than Gwen, was acknowledged to be both the oldest and wisest among all of us.

Daisy had lived at the Maury River Stables her entire life, and so had her dam. She carried herself as proudly as any Thoroughbred I'd ever met, and that intrigued me. I calculated that she could teach me what I needed to know, but I suspected there would be an extensive price to pay.

Upon my honor, I truly wanted to do right by Ashley, and Mrs. Maiden, too, but I didn't know how to start. Anyway, I wasn't about to go groveling to a pony by asking for help.

The truth is I didn't know how to befriend a mare or

a gelding. People were a might easier, especially if they were ones like Filipia and John, with their stories and songs, and hearts as full of shadows and light as mine. That's why I liked them, I supposed, but never had I lived with a horse or pony who really understood me, not even Marey.

I caught a whiff of new grass, overlooked up to that point. The Welsh stuck her muzzle through the fence slat on my side and pulled at the sweet clump. Our eyes met, and for just a flash, I caught a possibility that the Maury River Stables might could be a different sort of place, where I might could become a different sort of horse.

"Do you care to share, or do you plan on taking all that for yourself?" is what came out of my mouth. Not the finest offer of friendship, but there it was.

Daisy didn't even acknowledge me or say anything. A powerful urge was building in me to try something new, like make a friend, but I had nothing. Daisy returned to grazing on the mare side.

CHAPTER THIRTY-THREE

A Word

Turns out Daisy herself took care of initiating a conversation during our next visit at the fence line. Every mare I've ever met thinks she knows what's best for me. Daisy was no different.

One evening after Ashley and I had worked together under saddle, Daisy called me over.

"Dante, a word," she said.

Of course, the Welsh was in no way the boss of me, but if I had learned a lick of a lesson about anything, I figured after my initial display of poor manners, I ought to at least give some sort of tribute to this pony. I didn't intend on obliging her every little demand, but no harm in pretending to listen. I made my way toward her, stopping along to nab assorted grasslings and sproutlings.

She stomped her foot for me to hurry up. "This is no trivial matter. You and I've got business to discuss. If you don't care to give Mrs. Maiden and the children your best effort, you'd best move on to your next stop. And I hate to imagine where that might be."

I admit; she startled me. I grabbed a mouthful of clover and sidled up to the fence. She laid into me in a way that no horse had ever done, nor has done since. Soon as I reached her, that bossy pony turned on the forehand and proceeded to kick the tarnation out of the fence planks. The boards shook and rattled all down and up the line. Every gelding and every mare lifted their heads to look at me. Somebody whinnied. Not a one of them went back to grazing.

"I'd rather your hind end was the recipient instead of an innocent wooden board. You should be ashamed, and I'm certain your dam would be if she had any notion of the mean and angry horse you've become."

My muzzle dropped agape.

"Shut your hay hole, Dante. I watched Ashley try to ride you today, and that was the last time you will act out or put a student of ours in danger. Do you hear me?"

I was stunned. "I love Ashley. I'd never hurt her."

"Are you really blind to your own reckless arrogance?" Daisy was screaming at me. "You reared up.

Twice. The second time she came off. Then you refused to let her mount again. The child left our barn in tears."

I had to defend myself. "First of all, she had a crop in her hand, okay? I do not like pointy things. Second of all, Ashley cries all the time. Especially when she's mad."

Daisy slammed on the fence so fast and so hard that the top board cracked. I knew better than to run away. For one, everybody was watching. If I bolted, they might think I was scared of a Welsh pony.

When finished, Daisy had another question for me. "Why are you even here?"

I didn't need to think too hard about my answer. "For Ashley."

"Then grow up and be a horse. Stop acting like a wean. Your grain may run late, but it will always come. Some hay flakes taste better than others. People use pointy things: needles, pitchforks, hoof picks, and, yes, even spurs. My advice? Search your heart and decide who you are and who you want to be, Dante."

The boarded horses whickered. Even Napoleon nickered. So. Everybody agreed with Daisy. Well, truly, if that wasn't like the fog lifting.

I let out a big sigh. I had a choice to make. One: walk away with my pride intact and my head held high and risk losing another second chance. Or two: take the mare's advice and search my heart and try to make it work at the Maury River Stables.

✳ CHAPTER THIRTY-FOUR ✳

GOOD GRACES

Not a gelding nor a mare spoke to me for a whole night and day after Daisy scolded me. When I went toward the hay, they scattered. The water tub? Same. All the school and boarded horses turned their backsides to me.

I got what I had been asking for. They were leaving me alone, isolating me socially. Letting me know that I wasn't really part of the Maury River Stables. And they wanted nothing to do with me.

Daisy waited until evening turnout, after Mrs. Maiden had closed the place down and after the moon had come full up. She whickered softly for me to come over to her. "You could be a great horse," she said. "You have what it takes. I can teach you, and I will. And if you agree to follow what I say, you could be a leader like me."

"No disrespect," I said. "I thought Gwen was the lead mare."

"No, I am now. We came to a civil agreement after she saw how I put you in your place the other day. She's been a good alpha, and I love her, but things are changing. The Maury River Stables is bigger than just Gwen, Napoleon, and me. Mrs. Maiden is trying to run a real riding school. A new kind of leadership is needed. Gwen understands."

"She agreed, just like that, without a fight?"

"She's older now, and she tires more easily. Her job will be to mentor new horses, especially those working in the therapeutic program. That's a higher calling than lead mare, to tell you the truth."

She pulled some clover, and we grazed side by side in silence for a time.

"Why did you call me over here?" I asked.

"Dante's Inferno, I want you to stay at the Maury River Stables," she said. "And if you'll follow my orders, you'll remain here and our two fields will become a herd. I want you to take your command from me."

One thing I knew Daisy couldn't do as well as she'd have liked to from her side of the fence was to control the geldings. But I most definitely did not need the burden of managing that motley group of equines.

I learned pretty quickly, however, that the Welsh are a stubborn, determined breed.

Daisy sure was trying to convert me over to her version of the world. As if I had a choice, if I wanted to stay. I needed to fast-track my way into Mrs. Maiden's good graces.

I bowed toward the gray cob.

"You got it. Dante's Inferno at your service."

"Good! We'll start you off with the Shetland. Have you noticed how Napoleon prefers to stay near you?"

Seemed like I could hardly step to or fro without knocking into the little guy. Even though the pony was always under my feet, I liked him. Daisy had noticed the easiness between him and me, and she had a mind of shifting some of her Shetland duties over to me.

"Before you came, I would huddle at the fence under the stars with Napoleon. He likes a story at night," she said.

"I'm not ashamed to admit, I've become pretty attached to the Shetland," I told Daisy. "But I don't know many stories." I lifted my head and looked around to be sure I knew where he was. Right on time, he stood first in line at the hay, as Mrs. Maiden tossed in our evening square bales.

"No worries. You're in training." She flicked her tail. "Besides, I know some of the Shetland-breed tales.

I learned them from my dam, whose name was Fancy, only I called her Mabin. I can teach you my Mabin's stories."

In training? Learning stories wasn't hardly any kind of training. Not for a Thoroughbred. As much as I had taken a shine to Napoleon, the thought of Daisy thinking she could offer me any kind of training at all hit me like an insult.

Didn't she know what all I had accomplished in my life? I may not have won the three tests, but I was still a grandson of Dante's Paradiso, and in my glory I showed as a fine, fine racehorse.

I walked over to the cedar tree to think a minute. What Daisy was suggesting was mares' work.

"I'm a racehorse, not a pony sitter," I told her when I came back.

"Correction, Mister Sporty-Sport. Were. You *were* a racehorse. What you *are* trying to be now is a school horse, so act like one."

I showed that mare my backside like I never intended to turn my face around to her again.

"Go right along playing like you're ignoring me, but you'd better listen. You could be a great leader. You have what it takes, but you lack discipline, focus, and drive. I can teach you, and I will. If you agree to do as I say."

As the sun disappeared behind Saddle Mountain, the temperature dropped, too, and all the geldings settled in for the night. On summer turnout, we spent the dark hours under the stars. Like he had started doing every evening, the Shetland trotted over to me. Stuck right to me like a blanket of dew on morning grass.

The mare's words had really chapped my flank. Me, lacking in discipline? No focus, no drive?

I ignored Napoleon, but could not ignore the shift that occurred in my heart as he followed me around the field in silence, blinking those brown lashes, seeking some comfort, looking for a friend.

A heart must hurt when it's growing and expanding, the same way a heart aches when it's cracking and breaking. Mine opened just enough to realize that I had given that pony no good reason to show me such devotion.

Daisy, watching me from the fence line, tossed her head up and down. I caught her drift.

"Hey, buddy," I said to Napoleon. "Did I ever tell you about my first race? Not too terribly far from here, over in Charleston. Oh, it was a good one, too. Fifty-to-one odds in a field of thirteen two-year-olds."

He nuzzled in close to me. "That sounds quite exciting, Mister Dante. Like a lovely story I'd like to hear. Go on, then."

Now, agreeing to tell a pony one story does not erase a lifetime of pain and suffering, both felt and inflicted. But it's a start.

CHAPTER THIRTY-FIVE

OLD FRIEND FROM FAR AWAY

Want-to is not the same as can-do. Stretch as I might, I couldn't one hundred percent allow myself to trust anybody but Ashley. Barely tolerated even Mrs. Maiden. My bloodlines, the pedigree on file at the Jockey Club, will tell you where I came from, but I hadn't the first clue as to how to get where I needed to go or even where that place might be.

Ashley did her best. Everybody did, but they didn't know me well—by that, I mean nobody at the Maury River Stables yet possessed the tools to help me unify body, mind, and spirit.

After a while, my hooves had grown long and were starting to crack. Even though I wasn't in what I'd consider a habit of real work, Mrs. Maiden knew better than to let a problem take root in my feet. I wasn't helpful in that matter, either. I had kicked the shins of a few farriers that had tried already.

One morning after grain, I overheard Mrs. Maiden on the phone scheduling yet another farrier to come out to the barn. "We've got an OTTB out here who's pretty fiery. He needs a trim, but I'll warn you, he won't stand easily. Three others have tried and failed. They refuse to come back." Then I sensed a lightening of her load. "Well, I would appreciate your visit. Sure, I'll hold him."

It seemed the whole barn—horses and people—seemed, was about ready to give up on me, including myself, and each for our own reasons, when a miracle walked through the barn door.

My old friend John. Good glory, how I nickered when I saw him, and I would have cried had I been capable. Ashley was holding my lead. John reached his hand out to take me.

"Dante, you are a sight for sore eyes." A big grin broke over his face. "I love this guy," he said to Mrs. Maiden. "You don't remember, do you? Dante and I were locked up together. Behind bars," John said. "Right, boy?" He patted my cheek.

Mrs. Maiden's face pinched up tight. "Locked up?"

"Yes, ma'am. I won't lie to ya. I served five years at

Riverside for a felony offense. Nothing violent, I promise. Prison's where I met Dante. I met you and Ashley there, too."

John had brought a little low-to-the-ground dog with him. A corgi named Katie curled right up at Ashley's feet. Her friendliness got a good laugh and seemed to dispel the anxiety that might have been stirring up in Mrs. Maiden.

She smiled. "Oh, Bet's program? Now I remember you. You showed us Dante, right? You've grown a beard. I didn't recognize you."

"You got it," said John. He cut away from talking about himself. "I can show you a few tricks about him. He's as good as they come. Particular in his ways, but as good as they make 'em."

Ashley patted me like she always did, with a loud *whop-whop-whack* on my shoulder.

"See, that's how I know he likes you. He's letting you handle him roughly. He's dancing around a bit but not putting up much of a protest."

"That's rough handling?" Ashley asked.

"To him? Yes, indeed."

"He'll hardly let anybody touch him," said Mrs. Maiden.

John nodded. "Right, he's persnickety. Watch." John stroked my neck. "Easy is more his style."

Ashley copied him. I stayed as still as a blade of grass on a day without a breeze. Only sweet feed could've made me move.

"Are all racehorses nervous and crazy acting like Dante?" Ashley asked.

"Nope, every single TB is different. Has to do with their pedigree and, of course, how they were treated and trained."

"Bet tried to tell us that he needed a lot of work. I had hoped we would have made more progress by now," Mrs. Maiden said.

"Yeah, I hear you. Everybody wants a Thoroughbred today. Some OTTBs could probably trot right in here and get working as school horses. Others? Maybe not ever. Some are wound so tight from the track that they need to chill in a field for a few years."

"What do you think about Dante?" Ashley wanted to know. "Will he ever let me ride him without bucking and taking off? Or figure out how to do anything other than run fast and be mean to other horses?"

I understood what she was saying, but little did she know, in my younger days I'd have been vigorously protesting this entire conversation happening around me.

John took a sidelong look at me. "How's he coming under saddle? Are you able to work him?"

"Not really," Mrs. Maiden said. "Ashley longes him every day."

"That's good," John said.

"Almost every day. Some days I just groom him, but I've stopped trying to tack him up, even," Ashley chimed in.

John led me to the cross-ties. Bet your last bale of timothy hay that not a word of this talk was lost on me. While my old friend the farrier trimmed my feet, I stood for him without a lick of trouble. As best I could, of course.

"You know, I'm not sure he'll ever get to where he needs to be. I hate to give up on a horse, but maybe Dante ought to live out his life as a companion horse," Mrs. Maiden said.

John set down my hoof, and I already felt an improved sense of balance. "That'd be a shame, for sure. He's talented. He has a good heart. In prison this horse was my best friend. There for me every day. Who knows what all he's been through."

"Maybe you'd like him, John?"

He rubbed his hand down my back. "I wish I could take him. I really do."

"Seriously, I can't keep him at my school if we can't get him under saddle and if he's not safe," said Mrs. Maiden.

"You rode him a lot at the prison," Ashley said. "Would you help us?"

As he was done with my feet—and with appointments for the day—I lifted a front leg out to him. John broke into a big grin. He held my knee and laughed. "That's my boy, right there. How can I refuse?"

CHAPTER THIRTY-SIX

SHOW ME

With all the work I was doing, to tell the truth, I didn't have much time to act up. I was plumb exhausted. My new mentor, Daisy, had me running around the gelding field learning all the landmarks and fence lines: the hay ring, the enormous gray boulder, and the old stand of cedar trees. John and the corgi started coming out to the barn twice a week to work with Mrs. Maiden, Ashley, and me.

"Can you really help me ride Dante?" Ashley asked.

"I believe so. First off, let's see . . . do you have a peppermint? Very important."

Ashley ran into the tack room. Lo and behold, she returned with a bag of treats. She had been holding out on me.

"Like I said, Dante is finicky. Not all Thoroughbreds are as sensitive as this guy and not everyone would agree with me on rewarding him with sweets."

"Whatever works," said Mrs. Maiden.

He explained how I liked to know what was coming next, and how he always talked and showed me each step. He reminded Ashley to show me the blanket, saddle, and girth before placing the tack ever so gently on my back.

"So far, so good. Go real slow with tightening the girth. Yep. Now, give him a treat. Pat his neck."

Next, he led me into the round pen in front of the barn. Ashley followed. He picked up the longe line, clipped it to me, and pushed me out on the rail. Longeing had been a big part of my workdays since starting out at Gary's. My mind clicked into gear. "About ten minutes on each side."

"Oh, I haven't been longeing him for that long. He goes so fast, and he gets all snorty and prancy. I guess I get scared and stop."

"Now, don't be afraid. Be patient. He actually likes longeing, but you want to give his mind the time it needs to relax. Dante has so much energy that if you jump on and ride him cold, it won't work."

"Why? Other horses, like Daisy and Gwen, I could ride around bareback in the field."

John cracked up laughing. "And I bet you do, too. Nah, not this guy. He wants to go fast. All the time. But you don't always want him going great guns, right? If you ask him to trot do you want him to gallop?"

Ashley shook her head.

"Right, well, racehorses aren't trained to walk or transition slowly or make pretty circles. Dante here was taught one thing: Go, man, go!"

As I made circles around the group, I started to relax. I felt happy to be working with John again. Somebody who knew me and what I needed.

"There we go, Dante. That's it. Easy. Easy." My cue to slow down. "Do you see what we did here, Ashley, by giving him plenty of time to settle and not rushing him? A couple of things. Number one: we burned off some of his energy. Number two: we gave him something to focus on. Number three: we also let him look around, check things out."

"He's so much calmer now," said Mrs. Maiden. "We knew working with an OTTB would be different, didn't we, Ash? I hadn't factored in the peppermints, though."

"Now for the big test." John grinned. "Into the ring we go. Ashley, why don't you walk him to the mounting block. I'll hold him and give him treats while you hop up in the saddle. Well, don't hop. Just ease your way."

Though I knew Ashley had a bad habit of holding her breath, she was not a wiggly rider. And she felt calmer now that she knew what I liked.

"Nice job. All right, go ahead and lean down and give him a candy. There you go. Now, walk off. Stay soft. I learned that the hard way. Let him look around some more."

Mrs. Maiden watched all this, nodding her head. Ashley and I walked around the ring. I recollected our first easy walk at Riverside and started to relax. I let it all come back to me, and I felt Ashley smile.

"Now he's good to go. Just ride him normal, now. He'll be okay to work."

Ashley and I walked all around the ring. Naturally, Gwen, Daisy, and the other mares pressed themselves up against the fence, watching us from afar. I pretended not to notice. When Ashley came upon standing water from a recent rain that took up a full corner of the ring, she started to cut and go around.

"Nah, go on through it. He'll go. He loves water. Now, how many horses can you say that about? See how awesome he is?"

John spoke the truth. The puddle cooled my toes and relaxed me. I dropped my head and might have even groaned a little, it felt so good.

"I wouldn't have guessed that," said Mrs. Maiden.

"Oh, Dante's full of surprises."

"And what if we don't go through all that each time, with the longeing and the candy?" Mrs. Maiden asked. "If we forget a step?"

"Same results you've been getting. He won't like it. I believe he was mishandled over the years, but who knows? Really, all this is about trust and repetition, and easing him into work."

CHAPTER THIRTY-SEVEN

CALL ME SWEET

For the rest of the summer, my regimen consisted of rigorous daily longeing, flatwork, and plain old walking or trotting circles and spirals and serpentines. We'd walk then trot then come back to a walk. We'd trot then walk then come back to the trot. Once I had walk-trot down, we began to work at the canter. Then came even more transitions.

Mrs. Maiden was feeling confident that the time might be upon us to test how well I'd handle the environment of the show ring. After all, if I was ever to become a show horse for Ashley, I'd need to learn how to handle my business in public. Personally, I saw no big rush to prove anything to anybody. I'd have been tickled to stand in my stall eating hay, minding my own business.

But everybody's got to work.

With help from the Maury River Stables family, Mrs. Maiden organized a small hunter show at her farm. Kids, ponies, and equines from all over Rockbridge County came out. Mrs. Maiden's friend Stu fired up the grill with hamburgers and hot dogs. The moms served coffee, lemonade, cold water, and brownies. All spiffed up and ready to show, the riding students looked almost as pretty as their horses.

A rainbow of ribbons waited on display at the judge's stand. All of Mrs. Maiden's students and the parent-volunteers turned out in Maury River Stables polo shirts to represent the home barn. The show judge that day was none other than the neighbor up the road, Mrs. Pickett, who had grown up a hunter herself but now preferred raising donkeys, mules, and llamas to hunting.

Ashley planned to show three horses: Daisy, Gwen, and me. Ashley and I were scheduled for two classes: Walk-Trot and Pleasure.

While Ashley showed Daisy over fences, Gwen and I waited our turn in the barn. Mrs. Maiden had cleared out the row of stalls across from me for the day so that visiting horses might have a place to rest. The large turnout meant the show would likely continue through afternoon. That meant Gwen was in the stall right next to mine.

On a typical day, Gwen and I didn't have a whole heck of a lot to say to each other. Oh, she and I had exchanged formalities across the fence line on occasion, but not much more. The newest horse at the Maury River Stables was a Belgian draft named Macadoo. He had arrived not all that long after I had, and the Hanoverian seemed more concerned with helping him acclimate than with helping me. And that had been bugging me ever since he had arrived.

Macadoo would have his turn in the ring with a student named Eric and go against Ashley and me in our Pleasure class. To my view, Macadoo boasted nothing but a big body and clunky feet. He claimed to be a purebred, but no papers had come with him. Plus, he had a big chunk missing from one of his ears. A little rough around the edges is what I'm saying. I wasn't too worried about the Belgian as a competitor, but I couldn't understand what Gwen saw in him.

I finally got up my nerve to ask her while we waited for our classes. "Now, Gwen, I know I haven't been here that much longer than Macadoo, but I wonder something. Why do you take such an interest in him?"

By that, I was implying *and why not me?*

Gwen dropped her head to pick up some hay, but she didn't turn her backside to me, so I figured she was reflecting on the question.

She took a long drink of water from the plastic bucket attached to the wall, then answered, "I suppose I've been trying to figure you out."

"Not much to figure," I replied. "What you see is what you get." I hadn't yet learned my lesson about smart-talking a mare.

Gwen let me have a stern piece of her mind. "What I see is a gifted and beautiful but spoiled horse who has a good twenty or so years ahead of him, yet who has neither learned how to be a horse at all nor relate to the people who care about him. I see a horse who every day fails to show any gratitude for the incredible opportunity he's been given."

I decided to paw myself into a deeper hole by making a joke. "Oh, I get it. You haven't talked to me much because you didn't want to have to be rude."

"Precisely," Gwen said. She put her nose into the corner and spun her tail toward me.

Now I was the one with nothing to say. I didn't even want to consider whether the Hanoverian might be right, but her opinion of me seemed a smidgen unfair. I was loading up to give her what for, but before I could mouth off too much, a horse mom walked into the barn and right up to me.

Straightaway, I realized she was Ashley's mom. I figured Ashley had told her which stall I lived in.

Her hair was curly like Ashley's and as dark as my coat, like Ashley's. She had the same big, round eyes and good long nose that I admired so much in Ashley.

"You must be Dante, the horse who's given so much trouble to my daughter. I wanted to come meet you. See for myself why she loves you so."

I didn't offer a whicker or a nicker or any sound at all. For one, because we had only just met. For two, there was a gravity to her tone that unnerved me.

On the surface, she looked like a kind and pleasant enough person, but there was something unpredictable simmering inside her. I prided myself on my ability to accurately interpret the true nature of people. For example, Mrs. Maiden's friend Stu always presented in scent and in spirit as a comforting blend of hay, grain, grease, and sweat. His earnest odor told me all I needed to judge his character: horses, land, and hard work. A man able to fix anything that needed fixing.

My friend John smelled like dog, horse, and grass. And peppermint. Also a winning combination.

The lady before me presented a confusing bouquet of fatigue and coffee, leather and chocolate. Not a whiff of peppermint.

Flummoxed at best, I pinned my ears. Just a mild

show of displeasure, since she was Ashley's dam, after all.

I'll grant her this, she was determined to make friendly. Without even asking, she slid open my stall door and scooted up beside me. I took a step back.

Thankfully, Gwen was now watching and offered some advice.

"Relax, Dana's a good person. She's not a horse person yet, but a good one. You could help her."

"You know Ashley's mom?" I asked.

"Yes, she's actually one of my students. A beginner. Tell me something, Dante's Inferno. You know Ashley as well as anyone. Do you ever feel that part of her is anxious? Or absent?"

Gwen hit on a true thing when she said that, but I couldn't ever put my nose on it till now. I had noticed how sometimes Ashley would just check out. I whickered.

"Those are the places inside Ashley that most miss her mother. Dana's been gone for months and months and has only returned home of late. That's what she does — goes away and comes back."

"How could she leave Ashley?" I remembered the first day I met Ashley, how she called me Monkey and told me how much she was missing her mother, this lady standing beside me now.

The woman scratched my ears; I shook her hand away.

Gwen snorted at me.

"I mean, where was she all this time?" I asked.

"She goes wherever her commander beckons. Ashley's mother is a warrior. I imagine that's why she's not afraid of you. I expect nothing much frightens her."

I bowed my head but kept my feet poised and ready should I need them.

Then Gwen surprised me. "Dana is like you, Dante. She's seen it all and then some. Here in the blue mountains, even though she's at home, the battle still wages within."

I could tell that Gwen was right. Dana's erratic heartbeat, her shallow breathing, and the way her left hand stayed tense, balled up, and ready to defend.

True enough, I hadn't invited Ashley's mom into my stall, nor had I initiated her touching me. Something Gwen had said, though, rattled me. The battle within. The battle she couldn't escape.

"Use your heart, Dante," Gwen said.

The same words Grandfather Dante had said.

"I see your pride twitching. I know you have a large heart that helps you go the distance physically, but your heart has a different job here."

"How can I help her?"

"By not reacting in your usual explosive, defensive way. You can help the both of you by stifling your distrust. Just accept Dana's touch. Try not to anticipate anything; simply be present."

I froze. "Like this?"

"Almost. Unpin your ears and set your back foot down. All the way."

Ashley's mom scratched my mane, and I instinctively let out a deep sigh. Then she did, too.

"Better," said Gwen. "You're no therapy horse, but better."

I felt myself dozing off and tried to fight it by asking Gwen, "How do you mares know so much?"

She nickered softly. "I've seen it all, too. I realized a long time ago that I could either seek out and surrender to the goodness in those around me or live my life as an unhappy, albeit gorgeous, warmblood."

Humility is, clearly, a rare trait among mares of any breed. Dishonesty, even rarer. Gwen was, indeed, a gorgeous Hanoverian. Her honesty and her beauty were a hard combination to beat. I decided to give her advice a chance.

I let Ashley's mom rest her head on my withers. I let my own heart soften. A horse with my bloodlines isn't born to be anyone's pet, but right there in that moment I found no shame in offering respite to a soldier. I calibrated my breath in time with hers.

I wanted to know more about Gwen's former life. She sounded as though she, too, knew something about hard work and hard knocks. So I asked her, "Were you a racehorse, like me?" I knew that other breeds besides mine raced, though none as famously so.

"Do I look like a racer? No, Mister Thoroughbred, I was a carriage horse in New York City, among other places. Later, a police horse, here and there."

"Whoa. You've seen the whole world."

"Yes, I have, and let me tell you something. I wake up every day and my eyes rejoice to see Saddle Mountain and my ears welcome the sound of the river, no matter how fast or shallow it runs. The Maury River Stables is a heavenly, healing place. A very good life for a horse, if you give us a chance."

Now, Ashley's mom may not have been a horse person, but surely she had learned some Horse along the way. No sooner did Gwen start waxing about the mountain and the Maury River than did the lady lean out my window and say, "I'm so glad to be home. I'll tell you what, Dante. Between you being so welcoming and Saddle Mountain forgiving me for being gone so long, I feel like I'm in church."

About then, Ashley came into the barn. She stopped in her tracks when she saw her mother. Her eyes flared white. "Mom? What are you doing in Dante's stall? I told you to be careful around him. I just asked you to peek in and see if his water bucket was empty, that's all."

"Oh, honey, he's a gentleman. What a sweet horse."

Good glory, I couldn't help myself. Yes, I did whicker. Nice and loud, too. I'd been called a lot of things in my lifetime: handsome, spirited, athletic, talented, promising, unfit, demented, intelligent, stupid, a head case, mean, and rotten. But never had any person or equine ever called me sweet. So I whickered again.

That day, Ashley had a pretty easy time getting me tacked up for our two classes. She took the time to longe me, and the work paid off. We didn't win, show, or place in the Walk-Trot class, but we didn't get DQ'd, either. I didn't bolt, rear, or buck her off. I did canter a little bit, though.

Surprise of all surprises, we placed fourth out of six in our Pleasure class. The credit was somewhat but not entirely due to Napoleon and his nemesis, a mule named Molly from over at Tamworth Springs, who chose that class to reinstitute their long-standing rivalry.

For me, a fourth in Pleasure was about as good as first.

"See!" Mrs. Maiden said. "I told you, Ashley. You two are making progress. Stick with it. Never give up."

Now that I had been called sweet and had even placed in a show, I almost had a reputation to live up to. I wasn't ready to admit to being spoiled or entitled, but the day had given me a lot to think about.

CHAPTER THIRTY-EIGHT

Fear the Night

A full day of showing and being on my best-ever behavior had wiped me out. I was ready to grab some shut-eye. We mares and geldings remained on evening turnout, but with a chill in the air and the light getting shorter, we all knew that the turnout schedule was about to switch from night to day.

The turnout schedule depended upon the air and on Mrs. Maiden. So any night could be our last one outdoors till spring. Sleeping under the stars made me feel closer to home and closer to the bloodlines, so I was hoping for a few more nights outdoors.

Best I could tell, the last of the show visitors pulled out of the Maury River Stables long about three o'clock. The students gave us our sweet feed in the paddocks, and then they left, too. We were in the field but for a lick when Daisy came trotting over to me in a huff, holding her head high in the air. *Here comes another lecture on leadership,* I thought.

She eyed the new horse. "I've been observing the Belgian. Macadoo could take the geldings over anytime if he really wanted."

"But he won't. He's too busy missing his old life. Spends his nights wishing on stars, not picking fights," I told her.

I looked around at the school horses and the boarders. All appeared calm and right in our pasture. Earlier, Ashley had emptied out the drinking tub, cleaned it, and filled it with cool, clear water. By morning, we would drink it dry.

Just minutes before turnout, Stu had chucked a couple of square bales into the field. No interlopers from the mountains — no deer, no coyotes, no bobcats. Not a stray skunk in the field. No loose children. No horses fighting.

All is well, I said to myself.

I accounted for Macadoo up at the boulder, grazing and wishing like he liked to do. I noticed that Gwen, on the mare side of the fence, always stayed close by him.

The boarded ones — Charlie, Cowboy, and Jake — were dirtying up the water bin already.

All geldings present and safe.

Except for Napoleon.

The Shetland was missing.

I scouted the field. He was not behind the cedar. Not on the great boulder, where he often stood to admire the view. I scanned the horizon and searched my memory. Stu had turned Napoleon out last, after giving us hay. Last I remembered was seeing his little legs trotting toward dinner.

One of my charges gone. Missing on my turn at the top.

I raced around the pasture whinnying. Angry that he was hiding from me. Afraid, when I couldn't smell or see or hear him. "Napoleon! Napoleon! Come out, now!" I commanded. Nothing.

I paced alongside the mare field and whinnied for everyone to join me at the fence. Soon, all had come together. Mares and geldings, horses and ponies, and the boarders, too.

"Who saw him last?" I wanted to know.

The Belgian spoke up. "Earlier, he was near the back fence, grazing alone."

"Yes, I was nearby for a while. Then I got thirsty," said Jake. "But that was a while ago."

"Search this field," I ordered Macadoo. "Go to

the gate and call for help," I told the boarders, for we needed everyone.

"Whinnying won't do any good," said Cowboy. "The truck is gone. Stu is gone. Mrs. Maiden is, too."

I pinned my ears. "I don't care. Get down there."

Cowboy trotted off. Jake and Charlie followed him.

Just then, I heard Macadoo squealing at the back of the field, closest to the Maury River. "Look! A break right here in the electric fence."

"He went through it," I said.

Then, for assurance that no other gelding would get the same idea that Napoleon evidently had, I bared my teeth and said, "You're all forbidden to leave this field."

The restless mares called us over for news of the Shetland.

"He's gone," I told them. "Toward the river."

"I'll go after him. I know the mountain," said Macadoo.

"I know the mountain, too," Gwen said. "I'll come with you."

Daisy interrupted. "The Thoroughbred will go. The Shetland trusts him. Only the ancestors know why, but Napoleon loves Dante."

Macadoo challenged her. "With all respect, Daisy, I've spent my life in the splendid mountains." He snorted toward me. "That soft horse has spent his life running in circles. He's hardly been out of this pasture. If you send him, I'll soon be out tracking the forest for the both of them."

Daisy pinned her ears at the Belgian, but Gwen defended him. "Mac is right about this, Daisy, and you know it. You're mistaken to send Dante."

Daisy pawed at the ground. Her word was final.

I pawed at the ground, too. Was I afraid? You bet. Afraid I'd never find Napoleon. Afraid Macadoo and Gwen were right about me. But I understood what Daisy was doing. She was giving me an opportunity to step up and be a leader who ruled by example.

"Boarders, keep calling for help," I ordered.

Daisy brought us all together. "We can't wait around for Mrs. Maiden. There's much to fear in the night, and our Napoleon is out there alone."

Macadoo whickered. "He's tough, Daisy. Haven't you heard Claire call him a demon pony? Coyotes would be crazy to mess with Napoleon." Macadoo tried to reassure everyone.

Gwen spoke softly. "Napoleon's not afraid of coyotes."

I had to admit that as his friend, I didn't know the pony feared a single thing on earth. "What is he afraid of?" I asked.

The Hanoverian lowered her head. Quietly, so that only the school horses could hear, she said, "He's afraid of the dark."

Daisy whickered at me. "He's always with you the minute the sun sets, isn't he? Always nearby," she said.

I had to agree. "All night he stands so close to me, up underfoot. I've often teased that he wasn't weaned properly, but I reckon it's no joke."

"He feels safe when he's near you," Gwen said.

I snorted my disbelief. "But why would a pony be afraid of the dark?"

Daisy spoke up. "I will tell you a story that my dam told me when I was a filly, but we must be quick. We're losing daylight."

I whinnied for her to get on with it.

"Once, on an island far away from here, across the ocean"—Daisy interrupted herself to explain—"an ocean is a great body of water, much, much larger and deeper and fiercer than the Maury River, or any river you could imagine."

"I've seen the ocean many times," said Gwen. "I grew up on an island in the ocean. Called Manhattan."

"Go on, Daisy," I urged her.

"Yes, well, you see, the Shetland's breed originated in the Kingdom of Scotland, mine in the Principality of Wales. Both of our native lands are cold, barren, windy places. One thing the Shetland Isles do have is mountains. Mountains with caves and tunnels. Deep, dark narrow doorways with openings enough that only a small pony can get through. There was a time when these small, devilish ponies occupied every cave of the Shetland Isles, hundreds, thousands of them peering out from burrows and hollows. Then came the dark years."

"What happened to the Shetlands then?" I asked. Everyone crowded closer to the fence line to hear.

Daisy hesitated, as if she couldn't bear to go further. "One day, men came to capture the diminutive horses. Most all of the ponies were stolen from the mountains, captured, blinded, and sent deep into the earth to serve the greed of man, pulling out riches from the coal mines. The ponies started out living in the earth and then were forced to stay there, many never to see the light of day."

"But what has all this to do with Napoleon?" I asked. "That all happened a long time ago."

"Not as far back as you might imagine. The ancestors that were subjected to this abuse live on in the Shetlands of today. It will take more than a hundred years over for the breed to heal from such suffering and oppression."

"But I don't understand," I said. "No one here would ever hurt him. What is he afraid of?"

Macadoo uncharacteristically lashed out at me. "Do you even hear yourself? No one wants to hurt you, either, but all you do is react to the harm that's been caused to you in the past. How can you possibly not understand?"

"Napoleon was never in the mines himself. That's all I meant," I said.

Daisy tried to explain. "Dante, the fear of the dark is in his blood. For many generations, the grands and greats of Napoleon's family lived underground in coal tunnels. Even Mrs. Maiden has learned to keep him in the sunshine. She doesn't even try to put a fly mask on him or cover his face. What she knows without knowing why is that he needs light at all times. Why do you think the barn is never dark? Napoleon colics when all the lights are out. So, you see? We all have bloodlines, for better or worse."

Daisy's story stunned all of us into silence, and I did finally understand. My own ancestry, my breeding, made me fleet of foot, and the Belgian's made him strong in back. The Shetland's made him fear the dark, and night was coming.

CHAPTER THIRTY-NINE

RACING THE SUN

Now, hurry," Daisy urged me. "You're in the most important race of your life. A race against the sun. Napoleon is small and vulnerable out there alone and very likely afraid. You know something of him now that few outside of his own breed will ever understand. Bring him home."

My fieldmates were counting on me. Napoleon was counting on me.

If I had doubted it before then, all doubt was erased. I loved the Shetland and would do anything for him, including swallowing my pride to ask a draft horse for help. "Macadoo, you're right. I don't know Saddle Mountain. Where do I start?" I asked the Belgian.

He pawed at the ground. "Use your ears. Use your nostrils. Those whiskers you won't let anyone trim? You'll need those, too."

The boarders took up their posts. So did the mares.

Macadoo, Gwen, and Daisy looked to me.

"I'll find our pony. I won't come back until he's found and safe," I promised.

The lick of the problem before me was this: all the other Maury River Stables horses had experience on the trail. They knew the river and the mountain.

Not me.

Except for the unorthodox hours I had spent in the Willis River with Filipia, my entire life up to that moment had been lived in confinement, of one fashion or another. A stall, a ring, a track, a trailer. Walls brought me comfort. A fence was as natural to me as the moon and the stars.

I had no skills, no knowledge, no nothing that I needed for this search-and-rescue mission.

Plus, plenty of time had passed since anyone had believed in me, and I felt a bit rusty as to how to handle that.

Though what choice did I have but to go forward?

Napoleon's stubbly, well-insulated body had

plowed through the loose electric fence and brought it down. I stepped over the cold fence ribbon and started down the path toward the Maury River. Mrs. Maiden and her students used this path with school horses to access the river for late-summer swims and to reach Saddle Mountain all year long. The trail was only wide enough for a single horse to pass. The grass alongside me had gone to seed, but it still stood long and dragged across my forelegs.

A bright, early star sparkled high in the sky, sitting below a shard of daylight moon. Opposing each other in the sky, the moon and sun hurried me along my way. Soon, one would take over and the other would take off.

The riding trail ended at the north bank of the Maury, which was running shallow that fall. I waded on into the riverbed, and my hooves sank down into the soft silt. The exposed pebbles and rocks allowed me to pick my way across. The water calmed me and helped me to focus. I paused and let myself acclimate to the river. I needed to think and to breathe.

So far, Napoleon was nowhere to be seen or heard or smelled. Not on the banks of the Maury and not within eyesight or earshot. Only a few little wrens scavenged along the river's edge, but no trace of a pony.

Right then, I thought about turning back, but

behind me I heard Macadoo whinnying. "Remember: ears, nose, whiskers! We're with you, Dante!"

The single star hanging in the sky glimmered brighter, and I thought I'd best keep moving, like the Belgian suggested. No time for fear and no time for a swim.

CHAPTER FORTY

CRABBIT

My prize for crossing the Maury was spotting a ferocious tangle of teeny-tiny hoofprints left on the muddy south bank.

I whinnied and whickered and whinnied again.

Nothing.

A few steps out of the river and the ground turned hard and dry, and it became impossible to track the Shetland any farther. Three trails branched out at my feet. One south. One east. One west. I figured that with my luck, the pony had wandered off into the deepest hidden crevice of the mountain's forest, so I took the southerly route down instead of the trails flanking east and west that went up and around toward the bald, exposed peak.

Fortunately, Mrs. Maiden and Stu kept the paths around Saddle Mountain navigable and easy to see with good footing. The mountain had long ago been logged. Back then, dirt roads had been cut to allow in trucks and dozers to seize the biggest trees. Breeds like Macadoo's would have done such work. Although the Belgian and I often butted heads, I'll admit that right then I closed my eyes and wished him with me, but I needed to prove to the herd that they could count on me.

Around the bend, I heard autumn leaves crunching and fallen limbs snapping. I dropped my head to sniff the path and, lo and behold, picked up a fairly fresh scent of hay and sweet feed. Napoleon for sure, I figured.

My whiskers came in handy, just as Macadoo had predicted they would. I sensed a subtle motion in the ground up ahead of me, so I hurried down the hill toward the sounds and vibrations and smells.

Then, I stopped dead. Because I knew if I didn't make the right decision, I might end up that way myself, and Napoleon might, too.

Oh, I saw the little fellow, all right. Not more than a tall tree's distance away. Ears pinned back and doing all he could to make himself invisible and fierce at the same time.

Trouble was, something stood between us. Not a beaver nor a bobcat. Not a coyote nor a fox.

The *something* was a black bear. By the looks of her, easily outweighing Napoleon. As hefty a pony as he was, this bear had him beat by at least a body. Maybe more.

Let me explain exactly how a horse who's never been on a mountain or in a forest, never explored a wild piece of earth, knows a bear when he sees one.

For one, the absolute fear that started at the tip of my ears and shot simultaneously to my eyes and my gut told me that whatever that critter was, posturing on its hind legs there between the Shetland and me, well, it was not my friend.

Horses are, as everybody knows, genetically inclined to make one of two choices when faced with a scary, unknown thing: fight or flee. And I couldn't fly away, even though that's what I was best at. Not without the Shetland.

Now, I had never faced a fight in my life. Not counting the pretending that Covert and I used to do at Edensway, and not counting all the dirty kicking and pushing and shoving that went on at the track. I could give as good as I got in my racing days, but taking up with a bear on its home turf was an entirely different test. I found a little courage and made a big diversion.

First things first. I whinnied with everything I had

to draw the bear's attention off Napoleon. A high, shrill whinny carried a message to the Shetland: "Get to the river. Get home."

Napoleon's one smart little guy. He didn't bother with salutations or formalities, but took advantage of the confusion.

"She's quite a crabbit, that bear. Lovely in her own way, but contrary," Napoleon cautioned as he galloped right past me.

I hoped to gain him enough time to reach home.

Now, I could see the bear had four legs—not altogether unlike mine, but shorter and stumpier. At present, she was pawing with two and standing on the other two. And further, I deduced that if I ran faster on four legs than two, then so did Mrs. Bear.

If I could keep the angry beast upright for as long as possible, Napoleon might get down the mountain and across the Maury. So I reared up, too, and that made me appear to grow at least a pony's length taller than that bear.

Just then, two little balls of black fur came rolling and tumbling out of the forest, down the bluff. The bear cubs—I admit they were cute—had left their hiding place to come see about all the fuss. I do know a thing or two about protective dams. Cute as they were, the little cubs provided two excellent reasons for their mother to fight to the death. She let out a roar that smelled like trout and sounded like thunder.

A gravelly growl of my own was rearing to get out. I let it fly and struck out at the bear. Believe me, she struck back. We danced around that mountain together, both of us on two feet, until I knew I had to quit fighting and start flying. A bear, I learned in an up-close-and-personal way, has got two things that a horse hasn't: sharp claws and nasty, sharp teeth. I never had liked pointy things. The time had come to flee.

I prayed Napoleon had safely reached home. The bear was throwing one heck of a hissy-tissy fit, and I couldn't hold her off any longer. I didn't know I had it in me to whip around in a spin worthy of Daisy, but that's what I did, and I retraced my steps at racing speed. Splits that would've astonished old Gary.

CHAPTER FORTY-ONE

LIFT AND HURL

The bear proved herself a grand runner. She gave a contest, all right. On the sunny side, I was as tickled as teasel to know that I could still move like lightning.

I didn't glance back once because I didn't need to. Her hot breath panted at my hind end so close that I used her exhale for fuel in getting to that extra gear and then some. On the gallop back to the field, I used my large heart for the purpose to which it was most familiar — working with oxygen, and lots of it. I burned along the old logging trail — hooves afire — and sent a covey of quail and a rafter of wild turkey scurrying down into a ravine to get out of my path. Not a moment for dillydallying.

I hit the Maury River only about six lengths ahead of Mama Bear. I learned two more things before the chase was over. Bears can run fast. And I can run faster.

Truly, sixty lengths would not have been a comfortable enough win for me. I tore across the Maury in about four strides. Left that bear on the south bank, glowering at me to come back and fight. By the time I picked up the trail leading to the gelding field, I was weaving around, breathing hard. I slowed to a trot, praying little Napoleon would be there to greet me.

As our pasture came into view, I recognized him standing there on top of the gray boulder that jutted out of the ground. It was too dark to tell a buzzard from a hawk, but I knew it was him standing guard. He started whinnying a greeting like I'd been gone for way too long.

Right away, I spotted a problem getting back inside the field. Evidently, enough time had passed between Napoleon's return and mine for Mrs. Maiden to stop by for night check and repair the fence. I figured now they were out looking for me. I just hoped they'd brought some protection.

Trouble was, now I had no way in.

I wasn't afraid of the dark, but I surely was afraid of being eaten by an irate predator. Although I was fairly confident that the bear had decided I wasn't worth the effort of crossing the river, I did not savor the idea of spending the evening all by my lonesome on the wrong side of the safety zone.

"You'll have to jump it," Napoleon hollered at me.

I stared blankly at him. "Negative," I said. "I'm a racehorse, not a jumping horse."

"I'm afraid you've no choice. None at all, Mister Dante." Then he added, "Come on, I believe in you."

Naturally, seeing how he looked up to me, I didn't want the frightened pony to know that I quivered at the idea of jumping anything, but a horizontal wire charged to zip-zap my tenders was unnerving.

By now, it was nearly dark. Napoleon would be needing his story soon, and if I could make it back to our field, boy, did I have a doozy for him. One I expected he'd ask for again and again.

I paced back and forth, trying desperately to figure another way over, under, or through.

The Shetland started to get restless watching me.

"My friend, have you not ever jumped before?" he asked me.

I whinnied; time to fess up.

"No problem, no problem. Not. A. Problem," Napoleon assured me. "A little help over here?" he called to the others, and that brought all the geldings and mares to the fence line.

Down the back line, all of them started to whinnying. Cowboy. Jake and Charlie. The Belgian. The
mares—Daisy, Gwen, and a couple of the boarded
ladies, Lilac and Princess. I wasn't convinced any of
them could help, but I sure had an audience. From the
sounds of it, the Maury River Stables' horses had given
me long odds at making it over the fence. My favorite
kind of wager.

"Here's what you do," Napoleon advised me. "Back
up a bit. Yeh, good. No, quite a bit more. There you
are, right. Now, pick up a canter, and when you get one
stride out from the fence, lift your front feet and hurl
yourself up and over, right? Lift. Hurl. Got it?"

So I picked up the canter. The bit about lifting and
hurling eluded me, but with the mares and geldings all
watching, I was determined to succeed. Just maybe not
on the first try.

"No, No, NO. Front feet up and hurl over. Really
go for it," Napoleon said. "Up and over. You didn't do
that part. You stopped cold, as we say."

I backed up farther down the trail. Seemed as
though I was the evening's entertainment, because this
time all the geldings and mares counted out my strides
in unison. From way far back they counted, "One, two.
One, two. One, two. One, two."

While they were so exuberantly carrying on, the
Shetland stayed focused on coaching me home. A few

strides out he said, "Get ready to lift your front feet quite a lot." Just as I was about to, he shouted, "Oh, and I forgot; push off with your back legs. Yeh, don't forget them, your back legs."

I slammed on the brakes and almost slid into the fence, all coiled and ready to shock if I didn't make it.

"Dirty stop!" yelled Daisy.

"Come on, fancy boy," Cowboy said.

"How's that pedigree working out for ya, Dante's Infirmo? Get it? Infirmo?" Jake was always trying to one-up Cowboy. I'd have to work on helping those two find a new place to board once I made it back into the pasture.

Napoleon hopped down from the boulder and waved me over with a front hoof. "Yeh, right. I see the problem. You're looking at the ground. Can't do that. You've got to find your takeoff spot—the spot that's close enough but not too far from your obstacle. When you hear me say 'jump,' I want you to lift—"

I cut him off. "—And hurl!"

"Right. And remember to push off with your hind. Now, back up. Quite a lot more. Still more. Really lift this time. Give it your all. Yeh, good, come on. Now, everybody count!"

All the mares and the geldings joined in. "One, two. One, two."

"Get ready," the Shetland called. "One, two. One, two. One, jump!"

I lifted and pushed and hurled myself straight up off the ground. Mares-in-heaven, if I wasn't floating like a bug on water. Up and over I went. Neither hair nor hide felt the slightest singe. Lo and behold, I cleared the electric fence. Not gracefully, but clean. I landed clumsily, all four legs splayed out in all four directions like a newborn foal unsure how he got there.

"You did it!" Napoleon started bucking. Charlie and Jake, too. "Scopey!" yelled Gwen. Cowboy reared up and brandished his hooves.

"Holy Moo," Napoleon said. "You cleared that fence by two feet. I mean, yeh, you fell down. You're supposed to land on all fours, and canter away with your mane flowing in the wind and all, but so what? You're home."

I hauled myself up off the ground and brushed myself off with my tail as best I could.

"*Holy Moo?*" I asked him nonchalantly. "Where'd you hear that?"

"Moo, that's my dam."

"Her name was Moo?"

"Yeh, I'm adopted. My dam was a cow, a Hereford heifer, actually. She never calved. She had her hooves full raising me up, I imagine. Plus, there was no bull around."

We had both worked up a good appetite and stood around the hay. Daisy and the mares crowded the fence line to join in the party.

"Nice work bringing the pony home," Daisy said. Before I could offer a whicker of thanks, she added, "But that jump? Despicable form."

My coat was still lathered from fighting and a bit wet from splish-splashing in the river.

"So, buddy, what made you leave today? I was half-way scared you wouldn't come back."

He had a big mouthful of hay dangling from his bottom lip.

When he finished chewing, Napoleon explained. "The electric fence looked saggy, and I like to take long walks. What with us going to be in at night again soon, I thought, *Now, here's an opportunity.* I like to walk the trails with the birds. Yeh, look at the birds. Waxwings, nuthatches, wild turkeys, and the like. Did you happen to see any good ones while you were out?"

★ CHAPTER FORTY-TWO ★

GREEN

As arduous as show day was, what with it being my first competition, my first venture up into Saddle Mountain, and my inaugural encounter with a bear, it proved also to be a turning point. Suddenly, I was not the horse with the problem but the hero of the barn.

Thanks to John the Farrier, I had started seeing a decent ration of treats come my way. Thanks to Napoleon, I was learning how to be brave. With Daisy's help, the geldings were under pretty good control, and Ashley kept up a predictable routine of working me on the flat. Life was good, and I wanted more. More ribbons. More praise. More peppermints. More friends.

As a reward for solid effort and good behavior, Mrs. Maiden gave us the niddly-nod to participate in a little hunter show at Tamworth Springs, not too terribly long past my seventh birthday. This time, Ashley and I set our sights on something bigger than Walk-Trot. I had come a long way since getting out of prison. The Tamworth Springs show would prove to everyone just how far. For this outing, we'd be going in Walk-Trot-Canter.

The best thing about Ashley? She wasn't scared of anything. She liked speed and power. Not once did I pick up on a riffle of fear in that gal.

Trouble is, hunters aren't really judged on speed and power; it's more about style and consistency. And keeping cool and calm.

On the upside, I will say that if there had been a class judged solely on being good-looking, Ashley Brooks and I would have pranced off with one of those fancy multicolored reserve-champion ribbons.

First-place blue was not to be our color at Tamworth Springs. Nor was red, yellow, white, pink, or green.

While Ashley wasn't a day in her life afraid of me, she was a nervous, quivering ball of upset on show days. One word describes her: shaky. As we got ready to enter the ring, where the judge would be eyeballing Ashley more so than me, my rider was a knot of nerves.

"Dante can sense your heart rate," Mrs. Maiden said. "Take a few deep breaths. Good. Now, roar like a lion."

That made Ashley giggle. I wished that trick had a longer-lasting effect, though, because once the class got under way, she couldn't remember any of the rules that Mrs. Maiden told her.

"Stay on the rail."

"Keep out of traffic."

"Be on your best behavior."

"Pay attention to your transitions."

Like I said, we two were impeccably turned out. Ashley's curly, long black hair was neatly pinned up in a bun and covered with a hairnet. Even though the judge would have allowed a heavier coat, Ashley was all about looking good. Despite the fact that we were all walking around in cold clouds of our breath, she turned out her formal dark jacket and crisp white collared shirt, both clean and well fitted. She carried a smart-looking crop, for looks, and wore brand-new black leather gloves. I had not a fleck of dust or mud on me. My mane was expertly and tightly braided. And that's a fact, for I did my best to rub them out. See now, if the judges had realized the heroic effort required for me to stand moderately still while they were being done — well, how about some kind of ribbon for style, is all I'm saying.

We got lots of nice looks. From everybody. I myself didn't spot a pair in the ring who could have racked up more points on style than Ashley and me.

Now, good manners?

Sadly, that's another story.

I never liked being crowded on the track. There, pushing and shoving and using your strength to clear out some space was an asset. In the hunter ring? Not so much. I imagine that's why Mrs. Maiden instructed Ashley to stay on the rail and stay out of traffic.

Listen, there's a whole advertising system that informs riders and spectators at horse shows of one particular thing or another about the horses competing. Tail ribbons, who knew?

Theoretically, if your people tie a ribbon around your tail, the color sends a coded message to everybody on course. Our fearless Welsh leader, Daisy, sports a red ribbon every time she goes out. That's because she kicks. Gwen, arguably the most regal among us, gets a pink one. But only when she's feeling moody or susceptible to the charms of a stallion. If a stallion were out there with us, he'd likely be wearing a blue tail ribbon of his own. Just because it helps everybody to know when a stallion is anywhere in the vicinity. Of course, there's also the white ribbon. Nobody wants to be flashing white, which advertises: this horse is for sale.

My green ribbon, woven into my plaited tail, alerted everybody that I was, in fact, a green horse. Inexperienced. Translation: this guy might spook. He might throw a conniption fit for reasons known only to him. Give him a break, and give him a wide berth.

At the show, I certainly did earn a few demerits in Mrs. Maiden's eyes, largely due to an incident involving one of Mrs. Maiden's youngest students, a girl named Claire. Let me start from the beginning.

Ashley and I had made a rats' nest mess of our class. I misunderstood all of the judges' cues, and so we actually rode our Walk-Trot-Canter class as a Canter-Canter-Gallop class. Impressive but noncompliant. As a result, we pinned a grand total of zilcho-zero ribbons. The only words Mrs. Maiden offered Ashley were "Why don't you take Dante back down to the trailer. Put his blanket on, grab your big coat, and then come back up here, and we'll talk."

Mrs. Maiden's directions rang as clear as Saddle Mountain, now that all the leaves had dropped from the trees. Nothing wish-washy about what she instructed us to do. We got waylaid on the way to the truck when we happened onto little Claire, who seemed to always be in tow with Mrs. Maiden, even when she wasn't riding or showing.

I could hear Ashley's stomach growling for lunch, as she was too nervous to eat at all before our class.

"Claire," Ashley said, "mind holding Dante for me? I'll be right back. I need some fries."

The littler girl wore a floppy wool hat with long, dangly strings. She tilted her chin and looked at Ashley. "But Mrs. Maiden said we would all eat together."

Ashley pulled rank on Claire and, frankly, turned a bit snotty, which I myself admit to doing on occasion, so I am nowise judging. Just saying that she intimidated Claire because she could. "Claire, I'm serious. Just hold him for one minute. I'm starving."

In hindsight, I suppose a safer plan would have been for me to stand still and unmoving until Ashley returned. Instead I panicked.

My intentions were true. I promise. See, things had been going fine and dandy for me for a good little stretch. In an effort to obey Mrs. Maiden, I made for the trailer and the peppermints that I knew were waiting for me there. Now that I think about it, I may have, possibly, dragged Claire along behind me. Knocking into chairs and tables. Bumping into dogs and people and the like. Though I hadn't a clue where the trailer was parked, I kept whinnying as loud and often as I could in the hopes that somebody from our barn might help a Thoroughbred out. Seemed like a good plan right up until the show secretary came over the loudspeaker.

"Isbell Maiden, please head over to the pavilion,

where your horse is wreaking havoc and making a little girl cry."

By the time I reunited with Ashley and Mrs. Maiden, a kindly whiskered gentlemen had ahold of me, and his friendly, equally whiskered companion had wiped Claire's tears away.

Mrs. Maiden packed up everybody in record time. We drove home to the Maury River Stables in silence.

CHAPTER FORTY-THREE

SOMETHING NEW

After our embarrassment at Tamworth Springs, where I had demonstrated that riding around politely with other equines was not my strength, in our next lesson Mrs. Maiden recommended a change of plan. "You two might enjoy jumpers more so than hunters," she said. "Let's give something new a try."

Little did Mrs. Maiden know that the mares and geldings had already given me my first jumping lesson back in the fall. I knew how to count out my strides and where to look for my spot. And I was well aware of the lift-and-hurl technique, though apparently I needed to work on my landing.

For my first few times in the jumping ring, Mrs. Maiden had us play Follow the Leader over little cross-rails that she set up. Napoleon would go over, and then I would go after.

Afterward, instead of story time, Napoleon and I would pass our overnights in the barn discussing jumps. We lived side by side indoors in the winter. He was a good friend to quiz me about what I had learned.

"Here's an easy one," he said. "What d'ya call the two tall poles on either side of the horizontal one that you jump over?"

"The standards," I said correctly.

"Yeh, good. Another easy one: if you just have one horizontal pole resting there between two standards, waiting for you to go over, what's it called?"

"A vertical?"

"Yeh, good. Harder one: you're coming down the straightaway and what do you see but two verticals in a row. And you have plenty of room between them to get in a few strides."

"Uh, I reckon that's two verticals?"

"Yeh, good, but you want to call it a line. Right? You see that? Two or more verticals in a line with some strides in between, just say 'a line.'"

"A line."

"Yeh, good. Harder: two verticals set up but you got no room at all to land in between. You have to jump the spread all together. What kind of jump am I describing, Mister Dante?"

Oh, I knew that one right away. "Why, that's an oxer."

"Quite right, an oxer. Hardest: you see you got a line of, say, three jumps with room to land and come up and go over but no room for any extra stride."

"A hi-lo?" Just a guess.

"Yeh, wrong. Look, what are you doing to get over those obstacles? Yeh, you're bouncing between them. Call it a bounce."

"A bounce."

"Quick, how many jumps make up a double bounce, then?"

"Three?" I guessed.

"Yeh, good."

Pretty quickly, I discovered that I liked jumping even better than racing. With just Ashley and me in the ring, and nobody kicking mud up in my face or growling at me from behind, we only competed against ourselves and the clock.

For the rest of winter and into springtime, whether we were schooling someplace new, working at home with Mrs. Maiden, or racing the clock in a jump-off, as long as were together and jumping we were happy.

Of course, our rounds would get compared to all the other teams, but when the time came to perform,

Ashley and I became a world unto ourselves. Just us. Nobody else. Until at the end of a clear round, when Ashley would smile.

Occasionally, Ashley would slice too close or turn me one hundred eighty degrees to pick up a rollback, and I'd hear a gasp from the crowd. Or some busybody would say under his breath how lucky Ashley was that I was a point-and-jump horse.

Believe me. I know the truth about myself. Ashley was a good jumper, but more important to me than how accurate she was with this aid or that yield was that Ashley was good to me. So I tried to be good right back to her. I'll say this: we never quit. By the end of our first summer season, we became the junior pair to beat.

For weeks, Ashley and I prepared for our biggest show yet, at a highfalutin barn on the other side of the blue mountains, where horses would come from all around.

CHAPTER FORTY-FOUR

A RECKLESS TRIP

At our big show, Ashley and I completed our first course of twelve jumps early in the morning. The crowd was getting settled with their coffee and crullers. Mrs. Maiden was helping the younger students tack up, so Ashley and I were left to our own devices to prepare for our speed round.

We liked working on our own. Ashley planned to longe me a bit to burn off some energy, but as she clipped on the longe line, the gatekeeper yelled over, "Number three-two-six? You're two rides out!"

"Never mind," Ashley muttered. "Let's get up there."

Our warm-up was quick. We trotted a loop around

a small sandy area once in each direction, then rushed into a canter.

We galloped to the vertical and took off long, soaring over the fence. With an equally strong approach to the oxer, we launched nearly a stride before the jump, and my hind leg knocked the back rail. She took me over a couple more fences, and then we felt ready.

Ashley nudged me over to the ring so we could watch the pair riding before us. The hay I had left back at the trailer was calling to my stomach. I was ready to ride and eager to finish my lunch.

A small buckskin horse, almost a pony, really, was being piloted around by a young boy of maybe ten, a bit older than little Claire, a good bit younger than Ashley.

No threat from those two, I thought. I could tell Ashley felt that way, too, by the way her breathing stayed even. This was all about going fast, and they weren't even galloping.

Suddenly, it was our turn.

"Number three-two-six in for their speed round. Dante's Inferno is owned by Maury River Stables. Ashley Brooks has the ride."

I snorted as we entered the ring, just for effect. I was jigging and prancing, and I knew Ashley felt me coiled under her, poised to attack the jumps. Skipping a trot, we moved right into a canter, or maybe it was a gallop, as we waited for the signal to go.

The buzzer sounded. We flew toward number one, a simple square oxer. Ashley closed her leg and asked for the spot, but it was too long.

A half stride later, we were so out of sync that I had to throw myself over the jump. I heard a couple people in the grandstand gasp.

Ashley fell forward, unbalanced and tipping to the left. She quickly sat up and pulled me right, aiming us at the next jump. The skinny red jump had scared most of the day's horses, but I sailed over it, of course. None of those jumps scared us.

The third jump was a combination. Vertical–two strides–oxer. I was pretty sure I could hear that timer ticking, so I ran faster. The dust shot out from behind my legs, and I imagined other colts behind me, ducking and shaking their heads as my clumps of sand and mud peppered their legs and faces.

I felt Ashley's body shift, and I tuned back in. No colts. No jockeys. Just the girl, me, and the clock. I went long to the next jump, eager to prove myself to everyone.

Ashley knew she needed to pull me up in the two stride, but we were flying high, and I took off after one. I knew straightaway that I had jumped Ashley out of the tack. My feet knocked the fence, but somehow cleared it. I hadn't lost her, so I kept going.

We galloped and twisted and turned to the next few jumps, and I heard more gasps from the crowd.

"Just four more," Ashley said as we approached the number eight combination: oxer–one stride–vertical. I soared over the oxer, but got in too deep, coming nearly to a stop. Bounce. I had to bounce. That one was reminiscent of the old lift-and-hurl episode over the electric fence, probably even a little uglier.

Ashley muttered a curse and apologized for landing so hard on my back. We both hated combinations.

From outside the ring, Mrs. Maiden called out, "Ashley!" as we galloped up to the next fence.

She must know we're going to win! I thought, so sure that we would.

A couple more close calls, and we finished the course without even pulling a rail. A couple of chippers, sure, but we went clean and fast. I felt Ashley grinning proudly as the announcer read our time.

Now that I had gotten a smidgen of jumpers, I understood everything. I wasn't meant to race. I was meant to jump. Jump *and* go fast. I never wanted to stop. Not ever.

But something was wrong. Mrs. Maiden came storming toward us, and I'll be honest, there was nothing lovey-dovey about the look on her face.

After that ride, I had figured Mrs. Maiden to greet

us with praise and a soft pat on my neck. I expected some warm words for Ashley. I had convinced myself that after the speed and power that she had just witnessed, Mrs. Maiden would be talking about the Horse Center, Culpeper, and Middleburg.

As Ashley and I left the ring we were met by Mrs. Maiden, demanding that Ashley dismount immediately and walk me to the trailer. I bucked little happy kicks to show her that I wanted to keep riding. *Forget the hay; let's keep jumping.*

"Wow," Mrs. Maiden finally said. "I didn't expect that."

"I know, right? We're awesome together!"

"Oh, you're something, all right, Ashley Marie Brooks."

Uh-oh, I thought. *Fun time is over now. In a big way.*

I kept one ear on Ashley and one on Mrs. Maiden. Ashley tensed up. Naturally I did, too.

Mrs. Maiden really gave Ashley what for. "You're lucky that neither you nor Dante was hurt. That was as reckless a trip as I've ever seen. In all my years of teaching or riding, I never." She shook her head and looked off toward home as if she wished we had never come.

"Did you longe him before your warm-up?"

A tear welled up in Ashley's eye and hung there. She had her chin tucked tight into her chest, so I couldn't see her face for myself, as she was hiding pretty well under all those curls. But I could tell a teardrop was trembling there, same as how I could tell that lump in her throat was growing bigger by the second. Same as how a big old rain cloud hovers, giving fair warning before it really lets loose.

"No, we didn't have time because they said we were almost on course. But I . . . I don't understand. We were the fastest. We had a clean round."

"I trusted you today, and you let me down. You can't cowboy your way around the course. Jumping is not all about speed. Do you understand?"

"Yes, ma'am."

Now, if you ask me, that's no way to talk to a dream team of a pair who have just jumped fast and clean. But that's Isbell Maiden for you. No holding back, no lies, no excuses. Toughen up and do it right, or don't ride.

CHAPTER FORTY-FIVE

THE UGLY WORD

Once we got home, across the mountains and back into the barnyard of our own Saddle Mountain, Ashley was as angry as a snapping turtle. Without a word and with a mile of tension on the lead, she marched me into the wash stall. She smeared liniment on my legs and back, and good thing, because my muscles were already beginning to tighten and ache.

My achy body was the least of my concerns. Ashley and I had really messed up. Mrs. Maiden was not inclined to let up on us. Not in the least. She said that our ride was dangerous and embarrassing. We didn't win, to boot. How did we only get third? How? And how in tarnation was the buckskin with the kid a whole three seconds faster than us?

I couldn't begin to imagine the answers and, by the tension sizzling down my lead rope, neither could Ashley.

Ashley and I would still have been crashing our way through bounces and oxers had Mrs. Maiden not uttered these words to Ashley at the top of our lesson the next day: "No more jumping."

"What?" Ashley screeched. "But, Mrs. Maiden! We finished third. That was only the first show of the fall season. If we keep jumping, I know I could have a chance at Junior High-Point Rider. Dante could win the Novice Horse Division. I'm sure. Please. I'll slow down. I promise."

Mrs. Maiden crossed her arms. "Ashley, I don't know what to do with you. I told you, this is not about riding slower. You've got to ride smarter."

"I will. Please."

Mrs. Maiden looked sorrowful when she shook her head. "I don't think you have a clue what I'm even talking about."

Ashley's tears didn't hold up this time. Drops the size of crickets started bouncing all around my feet. One of them struck my neck and liked to burn me up. Angry tears.

"Please, Mrs. Maiden. Don't make me stop riding. I love Dante."

Mrs. Maiden stepped up to my left side and clipped the longe line to my cheek. "Oh, believe me, I know you love him. And he loves you. You two could be a remarkable team. Could be."

"But what?" said Ashley, bawling like a lost calf in a hailstorm by this point.

"But. You both need discipline, focus, and knowledge. No more jumping is not the same thing as no more riding. On the contrary, I want you to ride Dante even more. I'd like for you to keep showing him."

"You mean, hunters? We already tried that. He's too excitable."

Mrs. Maiden rolled her eyes, then let out a belly laugh. "Trust me, neither of you is cut out for hunters."

Then Isbell Maiden uttered the absolute worst word I ever heard: "Dressage."

Mrs. Maiden forbade us to jump until we learned whatever lesson it was she wanted us to learn. We were seething. For the first time in a long time, I dreaded getting back to work — and with good reason.

Dressage.

CHAPTER FORTY-SIX

GET ON

The next day Ashley walked up to me, sulking even more than the day before. She rubbed around my eyes. "Sorry, boy," she said.

My least favorite words.

"Let's get through this and make Mrs. Maiden happy, so we can jump again soon," she said.

She tacked me up as usual. Before she put my bridle on and started with the whole peppermint-longe-peppermint-peppermint routine that I had come to rely on, she sat down to zip her tall boots, but this time I watched her fasten spurs around them.

This wasn't going to be a fun lesson at all. Those spurs looked suspiciously hypodermic to me.

Needless to say, I was on my toes the whole way up to the ring. Ashley longed me for a few minutes before mounting, coming in carefully for the final girth tightening.

At the top of the lesson, Mrs. Maiden entered the ring accompanied by a woman. A stranger. Already, I didn't care for this lady. She clicked and clucked about Ashley giving me peppermints, and she kept staring directly at me. Staring hard, too.

"I want you two to get some good experience together, so I've brought in Vera Straff to help us today. She's a good friend and a dressage trainer from Albemarle. I expect excellent attitudes and hard work from both of you," Mrs. Maiden explained.

"Go ahead and trot a twenty-meter circle in front of me," Mrs. Straff instructed.

Wanting to impress her, we trotted the circle, and Ashley's hands seesawed on the bit. I knew what to do from watching Gwen, so I tucked my head into my chest. I could feel Ashley's pride and mine, both of us smug and fairly sure of how impressive we looked.

"Stop," Mrs. Straff barked. "Stop, stop, stop. All you're doing is pulling his head down." That new trainer really got after Ashley. She came right up beside me, grabbed Ashley's leg, and pressed it into my side.

"His movement needs to come from your leg and his hind end. *Never* seesaw. I want you to try that circle again, and this time use your leg to push him forward and into your outside hand. I don't want to see you turning with the inside hand."

I picked up a very intense sensation of heat from Ashley's face and, sure enough, that first tear to hit my neck liked to singe my coat. By then, teardrops for Ashley were becoming as routine as peppermints for me. We were a pair of highly talented, high-maintenance athletes, all topsy-turvy and out of sync. But we didn't quit.

Again moving me into a trot, I felt Ashley press her leg against me, asking me to move differently. Ignoring this because I didn't care for it a lick, I trotted the circle with my head up and moved my legs faster.

Mrs. Straff shouted, "Ashley, you have spurs. Use them. He's just running out from under you."

She pressed her spur into me, and I tossed my head. What on earth was Ashley doing to me? She didn't back off, and after tossing my head and kicking out a couple times, I launched into a series of teeny-tiny bucks. Tit for tat, because that really hurt, Ashley needed to stop, and this was not part of our bargain. When she didn't stop, I came up with more force. Not quite a lift and hurl, but close.

"Dante!" Ashley screamed.

"I can see he has never been in front of or responsive to your leg. Make him keep going forward."

The spurs returned, and, trust me, I was done with that. I stopped and did something I hadn't done in quite some time.

I reared.

And I reared, and I reared.

I came back to the ground snorting and all fired up and foaming at the jowls. Pretty quickly, though, I felt ashamed, for I could feel Ashley up there in the saddle shaking like December's last lone sycamore leaf shivering and quivering over the Maury River.

I knew she was going to get those spurs off of me sooner or later. Sooner, I hoped. I figured we'd make up when we were eye to eye, after she apologized. I really didn't, and still don't, like pointy things.

Suddenly, Ashley smacked my rump with her crop, an accessory she had often carried but never utilized. And with an attitude I'd never heard from her before, she said, "Get on, Dante."

Her tone smarted about as much as the whip. There was no getting through to her. All around the circle, she pushed me with her leg and voice and one more tap with the crop. Her hands held the bit on the outside, and she pressed her legs to turn me.

Here's the big surprise. Mares-in-heaven, the bit had never felt so good in all my life.

I chewed and moved my mouth around on the bit, and as Ashley relaxed little by little, so did I. My back was swinging loosely with every step, and I pushed myself forward on every stride. Ashley's back straightened, and her leg encouraged and aided me.

I can truly say that for half a circle, we floated. Just like swimming in the river. And then her leg came off, and her hand stayed on. Feeling the support leave, I immediately walked, then stopped.

Everybody stood there in stunned silence. Ashley and I most of all. We were shocked by what we had felt, and our teachers were surprised by what they had seen.

"Well, Isbell. You didn't tell me he could move like that," said our dressage sergeant, Mrs. Straff. To Ashley and me, she said, "You passed the first test. Let's keep working."

CHAPTER FORTY-SEVEN

CUTE PAIR!

I'll admit I was surprised the next morning when Ashley actually showed up for our second dressage lesson, this one with Mrs. Maiden.

Of course, I liked Ashley a lot. She was a good rider. Willing, eager, and obedient.

That's right, obedient. Up until our meeting with Mrs. Vera Straff, Ashley always did what I asked and what I wanted. She let me decide and never gave me an ounce of trouble at all. Sure, every now and again she'd swat me on the rump or the shoulder. Once, I mistakenly stomped her foot. She apologized.

"Oops, sorry, Dante. Move, please."

No complaining from her at all. For the most part, she also was a balanced rider. I never had to worry much about her coming off me. Her legs stayed steady and even. Looking back, I can say that the problem wasn't only Ashley, but it wasn't all me, either. It was us together.

After weeks and weeks of practice on the flat, Ashley and I still struggled. Mrs. Maiden framed the trouble exactly.

"Ashley, do you have any idea why I put a stop to you and Dante in jumpers for now?"

All too fast, Ashley checked out. "No, ma'am."

Even I had learned around Mrs. Maiden that you had to at least pretend to try. If a student complained too much about the heat or the cold or being tired or sore, Mrs. Maiden would say, "Take my advice: fake it till you make it."

Ashley should have heeded those words.

Now, Mrs. Maiden didn't get too riled up. She didn't raise her voice or flap her arms, but the tone in her voice turned as chilly as dawn in December. A sure-enough reminder that winter had arrived.

Mrs. Maiden asked the question again. Pretty clearly giving Ashley a second chance. Mrs. Maiden liked to give everybody a second chance. "Think about it. Why would I ask you to stop jumping?"

Ashley shrugged.

Uh-oh, Ashley, I thought. *There's nothing Mrs. Maiden hates worse than not even trying.*

Ashley stood to my left, her posture drooping and her eyes avoiding. I snapped her with my tail to wake her up a little bit.

She looked at me and smiled. "Stop, Dante."

I stomped my foot, and she laughed.

"Here's exactly why. Who's in charge of this situation?"

"What do you mean?"

"What I mean is, who is making the decisions out there?"

Nothing from Ashley. Not an eyebrow lift, not a chin tilt, not half an answer lodged in her throat nor a cough to bring it up and out and into the open.

"Dante, your horse, is in charge," Mrs. Maiden said, and did she ever sound frustrated. "You're letting him make the decisions. He's happy to do it, most of the time, but I'll tell you right now, there's nothing more dangerous."

Ashley sure raised her eyebrows then.

"You need to be the leader. You're a good little rider, but you need to get smarter. You give up too much. Your horse tries to help you out. He'll jump, all right. Long, short, he'll find some kind of spot, somehow or another. But that's not fair. You have to help him."

Ashley's bottom lip started a-quivering, and Mrs. Maiden softened her eyes.

"Why in heaven's name are you crying? This is nothing to cry over. You just have some work ahead of you."

So, we got to working. Ashley came back, and we practiced until the ride was second nature to both of us.

Twice a month, Mrs. Straff drove across the mountains to get after us for a good solid hour. Most days, Ashley and I walked around so sore that we both needed lotions and ointments to ease the deep pain in our muscles.

Finally, after much consultation and after hundreds of circles and transitions, changes of rein, and straight center lines, Mrs. Maiden and Mrs. Straff agreed it was time to ride our first official test: Introductory Level Test A.

Back to walk-trot, but this time with focus and rhythm and roundness. We hoped.

By then, a new year had opened up and, with it, the hope of knowing beyond certainty that even though I was not a champion racehorse, I would have a forever home at the Maury River Stables. I had just turned eight and was embarking on a second career.

For my first dressage outing, we'd trailer over to Tamworth Springs to try to redeem ourselves.

"If you see that mule Molly, tell her I said she's a real stinker, and she's got long ears," Napoleon said.

Turns out, the Belgian had practically been raised by the Tamworth Springs mule. He came to her defense. "She's like a mother to me," Macadoo said. "She taught me everything I know about Saddle Mountain and the river."

Napoleon taunted him. "You're quite a clumper yourself, Mac."

I left the two of them swapping insults and chasing each other around the field. And enjoying every stride, by the looks of it.

At our first dressage show, Ashley did her job before tacking me up. Peppermints and longeing ruled the day, and we took plenty of time in the practice arena.

Mrs. Maiden, Dana, and Claire drank hot chocolate and watched us warm up. Everyone was in good spirits, including Ashley and me. We'd put in a lot of hours and effort, and today was our day to shine.

I thought our outing would be a cinch, because no single component of the dressage test we planned to ride at Tamworth Springs presented a challenge. Matter of fact, the whole purpose of the introductory level was to give horse and rider a taste of the sport. Our job in Intro Test A was to show the judge how well we could move forward with a good, steady tempo, both keep our balance, and show that we could ride the pattern.

Technically, not much to this one: free walk, medium walk, working trot, twenty-meter circle, and halt through the walk. Not a problem, as Napoleon liked to say.

The judge sat in a truck with the engine running, keeping warm, at the top of the arena. I could hardly make out her face. When she was ready for us, she honked the horn, then Ashley put her leg on to ask for a working trot. We circled the outside of the ring once, entered at the trot, and halted square, facing the truck where the judge waited to evaluate our every move. Ashley bowed her head and extended her right arm down through her fingertips in a formal, crisp dressage salute.

Throughout the entire test, Ashley didn't speak. She wasn't allowed to make any noise. She had to do all her talking with her spurs, her seat, and her hands. We didn't keep ourselves in that good river-floating place for every step of Intro A, but we had some smooth moments where we moved like the Maury. With the final halt and salute, Ashley broke her silence. "Good boy, Dante." She patted my neck, and our Maury River Stables family clapped politely. Dressage folks don't hoot and holler, but I know our people wanted to.

After the test, we all huddled up together to keep warm. We waited, then waited some more to get our results. I ate hay and let Claire practice leading me around, which went better than the first time.

Finally, Ashley stood beside me, silently reading our scores and the judge's comments. Now, I am a horse of many talents, but I cannot read.

I stomped once.

I pawed.

Then I lifted my hoof up to get her attention.

"Dante, what?"

I pushed my head into her arms, nudging her to get on with the sharing.

Finally, Mrs. Maiden seemed to read the one thing that wasn't getting read: my mind! "Read the test out loud, Ashley. So we can all hear."

Ashley took in a deep breath. "All sixes, one seven, and one eight." She scrunched up her face.

"That's wonderful!" Mrs. Maiden said. "Those are terrific scores for your first time out there."

Ashley made a face. "But listen to this: 'Stiff through turn. Needs more supp. Hollow. Fussy in contact. Rider needs to relax so he will relax. Keep trying!'"

"Now read the compliments," said Mrs. Maiden.

"At the free walk, the judge wrote, 'Shows relaxation.' She wrote, 'Nice forward, fair shape,' for our twenty-meter circle."

"Let me see. Anything else?" said Mrs. Maiden.

"Umm, not really. Oh! This is good. 'Rhythmic entry, smooth transition. Talented, athletic, and opinionated horse. Cute pair, lots of potential.' Mrs. Maiden, what does the judge mean, 'more supp'?" Ashley asked.

"She means that sometimes Dante looked tight and stiff. He could stand to be more responsive, but we knew that. This is a terrific test. You should be very proud of yourself and your horse."

"I wish Dante could be my horse. I love him so much."

Mrs. Maiden put her arm around Ashley. "As long as he and you are at the Maury River Stables, he's yours to ride and love."

A wide and full smile broke across Ashley's face.

We hung around Tamworth Springs long enough for the results to get posted and to collect our pink ribbon. Fifth place.

Dana put her arm around Ashley. "Sweetie, I'm so proud of you and Dante."

"You're not disappointed in us for only getting fifth place?"

"Not even a little. I know winning is fun, but give yourself and your horse a little credit. Some days, the big victory is showing up and sticking with it."

"Really?"

"Really. In a few months, you'll look back to today

as the beginning of something special. I'm so happy I was here to share this with you."

"Me, too, Mom." Ashley nuzzled me, and the whole herd of them gathered around me. Mrs. Maiden, Claire, Dana, and Ashley.

"Group hug with Dante," Dana said. They all laughed.

I closed my eyes and couldn't help but let out a big old sigh. I knew there'd be fresh hay waiting in the net when we got back to the trailer, but, for once, I was in no hurry to be anyplace else.

CHAPTER FORTY-EIGHT

DISCIPLINE

We got back to business in the dressage ring. Ashley improved with her aids. I improved in my listening. Mrs. Straff kept coming, and our work got even harder. After every lesson, the soreness in my muscles lasted a good long three days. At least.

Throughout the spring and into early summer, nobody even mentioned jumping or showing. Junior Horse Trials at Lexington was on the horizon. I know because Ashley was begging for us to go. She could hardly talk about anything else.

We hadn't jumped a single fence since the fiasco, but Ashley was serious about going to the starter horse trials in September, where jumping would be two of the three disciplines we'd have to master.

"Please, Mrs. Maiden! We've gotten so much better at dressage."

"You think you could handle him for all three components of eventing? Dressage, stadium jumping, and cross-country?"

"I know I could. Now that he's listening and responsive to my leg. Now that I know how to ask him for what I need. We know dressage. We know how to jump."

"You've got a lot of work ahead of you if you want to go to the Junior Horse Trials. He's never been cross-country. We don't even have those kinds of jumps here."

"We could build them! Please?"

Three days later, thanks to Stu and the riding school students, we had an open field with eight more or less natural obstacles set up for practice. The new Maury River Stables cross-country course was shorter in distance than any competition course we'd face, but it worked a whole lot better than nothing. In our home-style version we'd start off with a single log jump. From there, we'd breeze past an old hay ring, roll back and over the brush jump made of fallen tree limbs, then bend to take a hay bale–two strides–double log combination. Up the hill over an old picnic-table bench; down the hill over another. Back around the hay ring, over some vertical brush, and then pick up speed toward the last combination — a bounce of tire jumps.

Having been up Saddle Mountain, I knew well all the threats and dangers that we potentially faced out there in the open field. No two ways about it, the cross-country course gave me the heebie-jeebies, the willy-nillies, and the creepy-crawlies. On more than one occasion, Ashley had to smart me with the whip just to get me to agree to go.

Mrs. Maiden had yet to make any promises about whether or not we could enter the horse trials, but all signs pointed to yes. She started reminding Ashley to find and clean her show clothes. And they started worrying out loud about whether I'd let them braid my mane or not.

Even though we didn't have a firm green-means-go light, our training shifted from learning to practice. Practice with a goal in sight, if not on the actual calendar. In our dressage lessons, we rode a full test, from centerline entry to final salute. Mrs. Maiden put up new dressage letters that would guide our pattern. She turned half the riding ring into a makeshift dressage arena and the other half into a stadium course. The attention paid to every fine detail reminded me of the old days, right before a race. Mrs. Maiden even whipped out a clipboard of her own to make notes of our progress.

My previous life was lodged there in my memory, all right, but it rarely broke through the surface. Doctor Tom and Red, Mrs. Eden and Melody, Gary and Filipia, and, of course, Marey. But none of that felt like me any longer. I was so busy listening and practicing, and so tired—more than once I fell asleep with my muzzle in my dinner bucket—that I hardly had a minute to remember my racing days.

As we neared the date of the Junior Horse Trials, Ashley returned to school and came out to the barn every day afterward. We switched between practicing our dressage, jumping in the ring, and negotiating our way through the homemade cross-country course— my least favorite, even more so than dressage.

The only reason I could even tolerate that part of our training at all was that Ashley used her ingenuity to help me find a little joy in it. She thought it might be good for me to get used to going through water, since we'd for sure see that at a real-life event, so sometimes our entire afternoon of training consisted only of crisscrossing the Maury River.

"Let's go play in the water," Ashley would say. I loved those words dearly. Best believe, I never hesitated—not once—on that cue.

"Look at him prancing and flicking those feet. I agree with you. He seems to gain confidence in the water," Mrs. Maiden agreed. "Dante, you are unlike any horse I've ever known," she said to me. Mrs. Maiden said that with a smile, too.

Ashley gave me one or two full days off every week. She came out on those days and groomed and massaged me. No complaints there, except when she also tried to sneak in a little bit of desensitizing of my mane. I knew she wanted to braid it up nice, in case we did actually go to the horse trials, but that wasn't happening.

Now, trust me, I didn't haul off and kick her whenever she started fiddling with my mane. I mostly had outgrown my immaturity in that way. I danced around a little, not much. Pulled my neck out of her hands. Bonked her with my head to send a message.

Mrs. Maiden increased my grain. My hay, too. Various supplements started showing up in my meal bucket. Fine by me. I was working hard every day and ready to drop at night. I figured that after Ashley and I made it through trials, then I might let myself reminisce about the old days in Kentucky. Until then, I was a single-minded off-the-track Thoroughbred.

We repeated our dressage test until I really was dreaming about twenty-meter circles instead of peppermint candy. We jumped oxers and bounces. We rode to the jumps with Ashley counting under her breath the whole ride. One, two. One, two. One, two. One, jump. We let the jumps come to us. Just like the Shetland taught me.

Every day. Every afternoon.

Ashley's legs got stronger. Her hands softer. I stopped trying to have everything my way. Not all the time, anyway.

Then one Saturday morning, Ashley got out to the Maury River Stables extra early. Mrs. Maiden started the truck, backed up to the trailer, and loaded me and all my accoutrements, as Gwen liked to refer to tack, brushes, show supplies, et cetera. We set off for Lexington, where Ashley and I were to make our eventing debut at the Junior Horse Trials.

CHAPTER FORTY-NINE

BE YOURSELF

Now, the Maury River Stables lies only about fifteen miles — even less as the crow flies — from the Horse Center in Lexington, Virginia. We pulled into the compound and were by no means the first to arrive. Seemed like everybody had the same idea to come in a day early to acclimate and prepare. Give ourselves time to work through nerves.

The horses at Lexington were fancy and their airs confident. I walked beside Ashley as we followed Mrs. Maiden to the cinder-block barn, where I'd be lodging for the next two days — one to get ready, one to go.

Instead of driving back to our home barn, Mrs. Maiden and Ashley brought everything I might need to get comfortable and stay happy: grain, hay, and shavings. Water, as much as I could drink, was on the house.

Ashley filled up two buckets from a nearby hose, and as I was quenching my thirst, a runaway horse came tearing around the corner, snorting and foaming and looking scared. Reins whipping, saddle hanging upside down.

I let out a good squeal, one in about the same range that I reserved for alerting the rest of the herd back home to when the boarders were threatening to revolt.

Ashley was quick to notice the runaway. I expected her to jump out of the way, but instead she darted out in front of him.

"Whoa. Whoa." She held her hands out wide. "Easy."

Mrs. Maiden had gone back to the trailer for my brush box and tack. She wanted everything situated and organized for the next day's competition.

That stray horse was badly spooked and committed to it, so he didn't take kindly to Ashley shutting down his escape route. He stopped, looking for the way out, giving Ashley an opportunity to grab his reins so he wouldn't trip and fall. Loose reins are a morbid accident looking for an opening.

Instead of settling, the bay reared up, jerking the reins from out of Ashley's hands and dashing past her with such force that Ashley fell down. Then, around the corner came a sleek charcoal-dappled pony, a little Connemara a squeeze bigger than Daisy back home. Galloping full speed away from something or somebody.

Ashley hadn't time to get up on her feet. I saw her scrambling backward toward the cinder-block wall of the barn.

"Heads up," a girl about Ashley's age hollered, a lazy stretch behind the action, just as the two horses came racing back our way—manes flying and reins dragging.

By that time, I was pretty darn frustrated at not being able to get out there and help Ashley. If there was one thing I knew I was good at by then it was bossing around ponies and geldings. Macadoo and the boarder horses gave me plenty of practice.

"Help me!" the girl demanded of Ashley. "Grab the gray."

Ashley, being ever so eager to prove herself in all matters of equine endeavors, gave her best effort, but the pony was having none of it. Rather than get knocked down or dragged around, Ashley let the pony take off again. She was right to do so, but that other girl steamed.

"Thanks a lot," the girl said. Then she bolted after the two horses. A wake of shouts and booms and barks faded after the careening runaways.

About that time, Mrs. Maiden returned to a mess of Ashley sobbing and sniffling and me snorting and kicking. Not the ideal frame of mind to head into our biggest meet yet.

"What on earth?" Mrs. Maiden looked confused aplenty. "Ashley, why are there tears in your eyes and rips in your breeches? Please tell me those are not your show pants."

So much for easing into the eventing environment. Ashley was a shaky wreck.

"I knew I shouldn't be here. I'm not good enough to show with these other girls."

Mrs. Maiden looked up the aisle toward the racket of urgent whinnies and angry shouts. Yep, those two horses were making good sport of their girl. I watched Mrs. Maiden quietly figure it all out. "Oh, goodness, what happened? Are you hurt?"

Ashley shook her head. "I couldn't even catch a pony."

"Sweetheart, that's not your job. You're here to take care of Dante and to ride."

"But we're not good enough to be here. Did you see that girl? She's wearing Vogel boots. Custom made!"

Well, Ashley really stepped in it with that remark. No more sympathy from Mrs. Maiden. I could have seen what was a-coming next from well across the pasture.

"She obviously couldn't handle her horses, and you're worried about her boots? Have you even seen her ride?"

"No, but did you see her horse and that pony? All braided and fancy? There's no way Dante and I can win against those kinds of horses."

I whinnied in protest at that comment. Had Ashley forgotten about my pedigree? I stomped my foot.

"You want to talk about fancy? Look at Dante!" Mrs. Maiden wasn't exactly shouting, but her voice slipped momentarily into high-pitched frustration. "Ashley Marie, you're the one who convinced me to go back and get Dante two and a half years ago precisely because he's fancy. And I agreed with you!"

"I know, but—"

"Nope, no buts. Do you know the lifetime earnings of Dante's Inferno?"

"Yes, $356,718."

"Exactly. Do you know who his mother is?"

"Two-time Horse of the Year Dante's Beatrice."

"And, let's not forget, who was Dante's grandfather?" Mrs. Maiden was really on a roll.

"The last Triple Crown winner, Dante's Paradiso." Of course, Ashley couldn't forget Grandfather.

"I'm sure glad to see you remember; I was worried there for a minute. I'd say all that makes Dante pretty fancy. But guess what!"

Ashley looked off into the distance. No doubt thinking about that sign posted outside the riding ring back
at home. $5 FINE FOR WHINING. I imagine she was hav-
ing a time doing all the fancy math it would take to add
up how much she owed Mrs. Maiden by now. Beyond
me, that's for sure.

Mrs. Maiden didn't let Ashley off the hook. "Guess
what! Fancy doesn't guarantee a win here or on the
track. Training wins. Practice wins. Heart wins. Sure,
fancy can help. Confidence helps more."

That moment of Mrs. Maiden handing Ashley
a bucketful of tough love is exactly when I started to
love Mrs. Maiden. I had respected her, listened to
her, and appreciated her, but watching her stick up for
me and for Ashley, when Ashley couldn't manage to
do either, gave me a new affection for Isbell Maiden.
Hearing her stick up for my bloodlines to boot? Well,
that clinched it.

"But how do I get confidence when I'm so nervous?
This show is different from riding at home, or even at
Tamworth Springs."

Mrs. Maiden shook her head. "No different at all.
Here's the thing: if you lose confidence, your horse will,
too. Some days are easier than others. Every day you
wake up, you have to practice believing in yourself and
in Dante."

"I do believe in Dante." Ashley patted my neck.

"Just not myself. Not when I see how beautiful and fancy and polished these other riders are compared to me." That girl in the custom attire had really gotten into her head.

"What are you talking about? You're beautiful! Dante is, too. Come on, he needs you to be calm and sure and firm in the knowledge that you can lead him. The only way you will ever disappoint me is if you give up."

"I don't give up."

"Remember when I pulled you two from jumping? You were quitting the jumps when you got there and letting Dante make the hard choices. He needs you to show him that we never quit."

"It's hard, though."

Like me, Ashley was resisting her own God-given and self-developed talent. I whickered and lifted my front leg up and out toward Ashley, trying to draw her near.

"Look at Dante. He wasn't bred for dressage or jumping. He was bred to go fast, trained for the track, and set on a course to race and retire. Now, here he is starting over. Do you think that's easy for him?"

"I never thought about Dante that way. That makes me love him even more. I just get so nervous, Mrs. Maiden. My stomach has butterflies, and my brain totally freaks, and I don't know what to do."

"You do the only thing you can do. Be strong. Be yourself."

"And then everything will be okay?"

"You know what? Even when everything's not okay, everything is okay. And no matter what happens, tomorrow will be a great day. You deserve to be here. Dante does, too. Who cares about boots or braids or even blue ribbons? You don't get today back, you know."

Ashley wiped her eyes and looked into those round and wise saucers of Mrs. Maiden's. "What do you mean?"

"Have I ever told you about my son?"

"Trotter?" Ashley asked.

"Yes, he was my youngest. You remind me of him. Not the way you look. He was strawberry blond, like me. Fair. Freckled. What I mean is, like you, he worried all the time. About everything."

"Really?"

"Mmm-hmm. You've heard the phrase 'he was born tired'? Trotter was born worried. I should have named him Fretter."

Ashley laughed. Mrs. Maiden looked startled, at first, then her eyes softened, and the faintest smile crested over her face and faded away. She shook her head, like she was thinking to herself. "He was a good rider. He could do anything: hunter, jumper, dressage, vaulting. More than anything, he loved the trail. He and Daisy and her dam, Fancy, and I would go off exploring our side of Saddle Mountain for hours on end. Trotter never worried on the trail. His natural habitat, I guess."

"I love trail riding, too."

Mrs. Maiden picked up a soft brush and began to groom my coat. "Anyway, after Trotter's accident, I thought about selling the farm. Every animal, every acre, the house, the barn, all of it. Thankfully, the people around me, my friends and neighbors, let me grieve. That's what I needed. They took care of the animals, bush-hogged the fields. Made me eat. Sat with me. Read to me. Until the sun came out, and I started to thaw."

"What did you do?"

"I kept the animals. How could I part with them, too? I did sell about fifty acres to Mrs. Pickett. With the money and after Daisy's mother passed away, I bought Napoleon, then Gwen, and then I built a new barn and fixed up the ring."

"How come you did all that?"

"I realized that when Trotter was riding, he was confident and happy and at peace. I knew the best thing I could do for myself and for Trotter's memory was to take good care of my horses and to teach children to ride.

I wasn't complaining at all, but Mrs. Maiden was

so transfixed that she was brushing me in the same spot over and over.

Mrs. Maiden finally put the brush back in the box. "What about you, Ashley? Why do you ride?"

"Dad brought me to your barn when Mom was deployed to the Gulf the first time. I missed her so much; all I did was sleep and cry. He knew that I had always wanted a pony, even though I didn't even know how to ride yet. I guess I loved horses so I wouldn't feel sad all the time."

Afternoon was quickly turning to evening. The Horse Center barn had settled into a calm, easy quiet. All the runaways were caught, the horses bedded down for the night. Music from radios and muffled conversations drifted up from the camping area that had filled up with horse trailers. Here, now there, the call and response of whinnies and whickers crossed the aisles. Listening to Ashley and Mrs. Maiden testify as to the depth of their love and appreciation for horses made me eager to show up. I knew I was setting on my best performance yet, and I intended to bring it all to the Junior Horse Trials.

"Just remember, you are not alone. You have a whole team to support you and be with you every step of the way. At the Maury River Stables we all help out," Mrs. Maiden said.

Ashley embraced Mrs. Maiden for a good long time.

Then she draped her arms around my neck. "Tomorrow will be a great day," she said to me. "I know Dad won't be here, but I hope Mom comes to watch us so she can see how happy I am when I'm with you, Dante."

They gave me an extra flake of hay to hold me through the night, then Ashley and Mrs. Maiden walked back to the trailer. I dozed on and off, eager for sunrise, I myself as curious as anybody as to whether I had it in my blood to conquer the three challenges of tomorrow's event: dressage, stadium jumping, and cross-country.

CHAPTER FIFTY

THE THREE TESTS

Our first ride was hours away, but before the night had fully finished, Ashley and Mrs. Maiden were in my stall with grain, water, my morning hay, and instruments of beautification. For as strikingly handsome as everyone liked to say I was, show shine was something else altogether. In all the hullabaloo of the previous day's runaway horses and Ashley's anxiety, we hadn't done much to get ready.

The Horse Center had come alive with the smells of coffee, sweet feed, and sugarcoated donuts and the sound of horse hooves nervously clip-clopping along the paved aisles between the barns. In the distance, I could already hear riders warming up.

"Heads up, outside line!"

"Passing right!"

It was only September, but the rising sun lit up an unseasonably early lick of frost along the grassy ridge in view of my stall.

There was no lingering tenderness from the night before; Mrs. Maiden got down to business. "There are forty teams in your division. Get ready for a long day," she said.

Ashley ran her fingers through my mane, pulling loose stray bits of hay. Surely, she didn't plan to attempt a braiding.

"I think we're ready. And if it's okay with you, Mrs. Maiden, can we not braid Dante? The rules say braiding is optional. Plus, you know he'll just rub them out. Or try."

Mrs. Maiden fluffed my mane up. "He looks a bit scruffy, though."

Mrs. Maiden grabbed a hunk of my mane.

I pawed at the ground to make her stop.

"Okay," she agreed. "But we at least need to even him up and thin him out a bit."

Don't know how, but I did manage to give Ashley a relatively painless five minutes to spruce my mane and bang my tail.

Ashley tucked her hair into a net. A few loose tendrils hung out, but that went unnoticed by Mrs.

Maiden. Then she ran a brush through my mane and tail once more. We got tacked up in our usual way: black saddle, black reins, white saddle pad. All in appropriate order: peppermint, saddle pad, saddle. Peppermint, girth, peppermint, peppermint. Slowly with the tightening of the girth.

Out in an empty field near the river of trucks and trailers, Ashley longed me in both directions before heading up the lane to the warm-up dressage arena, already full of horses and trainers. Every horse there was braided up and every rider impeccably turned out. We weren't at all unkempt by comparison—just maybe a touch on the wild side.

A crowd of people had already gathered at the dressage ring. As Mrs. Maiden had promised, our Maury River Stables family was there to support us. So was my friend John the Farrier and his corgi, Katie, scouring the ground for scraps of breakfast on a long leash.

But I got the distinct sensation of Ashley's heart constricting. She was searching for her mother. Everybody was talking about how in the new year, Dana would go back to fighting, and Ashley would go back to being sad. I knew Ashley wanted to make her mother proud before she had to leave again.

Ashley sat in the saddle, gripping my reins. Just before our test, I saw Dana running toward us, beaming.

"You're here!"

"You bet, my girl."

"Oh, Mom." She reached toward Dana.

"Hey, what's wrong? You've worked hard to get here. I wouldn't miss this for the world."

"I know. I'm so glad you're here, but I can't help thinking that you're leaving again soon."

"Shhh. Today's a happy day."

Right about then, I heard a familiar voice behind me. "I thought I'd quell the rumor that my show days are dead."

Napoleon!

I whinnied and turned to see Stu and Claire and the Shetland, all dressed up for dressage. There was not a horse on the property, myself included, I confess, that cut a finer figure than the pony did that day. Mane to tail, he was braided to perfection. His body was clipped, save for a thick lingering clump left on his rump in the shape of a heart — the only competitor sporting quarter marks.

He wiggled his wag at me, ever the show-off. "I can see you're quite startled, Mister Dante. You've nothing to fear, as Claire and I aren't competing against you. I've brought the little sprout so she can get some experience at a bigger show. We're only riding Intro A. Today's your day to shine, my friend. And a lovely day it is."

But there was no time for socializing.

"Number ninety-three on deck."

Our ticktock for the day was all set and about to start. First, dressage: communication, rhythm, and control. Next, stadium jumping: twelve fences for balance, speed, and athleticism. Finally, the cross-country course: a bit more than a mile of natural obstacles, all about pure speed and full joy.

Let the trials begin.

CHAPTER FIFTY-ONE

Open, Natural, and Free

With our dressage test completed to tasteful applause, and our stadium round clean and sure, Ashley and I prepared to face the cross-country course. We hustled back on down to the barn to make a quick change for Ashley and for me.

Ashley ducked into the corner to change out of her jacket and into a Maury River Stables navy-blue polo shirt. She added a padded vest, to protect her trunk in case of a fall, and, on top of that, our team pinny, bearing the number 93. She wrapped boots around my front legs to protect me from sticks and rocks and such on the course.

For cross-country, we could be a little more expressive in our turnout attire. We traded my white saddle pad for a camouflage one. As a tribute to Dana, the soldier soon on her way back to a place with gunfire and no mountains, Ashley and I both would be sporting camo for cross-country—hers on her helmet cover, and mine on my saddle pad. A small, private gesture of support.

Dana gave Ashley a leg up, and we were headed up the hill to the course. On our way to the starting box, Mrs. Maiden began doling out the advice.

"Don't worry too much about speed. You two will go fast enough without even trying. Ride a clean course. Give yourselves time to think."

"Okay," Ashley said from the saddle.

"Ash, I know you've memorized the course, but if you blank out, look at the flags on either side."

"Yep. Red flag right; white flag left."

"Good girl. Now, the entire course is just over a mile long. Remember from walking it earlier, you'll cross that creek at the bottom of the hill."

"Uh-huh."

"He'll want to play in the water, but give him some leg to get him through it. Then you'll come back through the water after the stone wall. On the second pass, you know him, he's likely to ask to splash around and play again."

Ashley flashed her crop. "Tap, tap, tap."

"Exactly," said Mrs. Maiden. "Y'all are ready."

I started prancing around. Enough of the jibber-jabber. We had been training and working for months. Honestly, I felt like my whole topsy-turvy life had led me right here to this hilltop. I knew I had exactly what I needed to win: speed, power, confidence, and a rider who believed in me. I hoped she believed in herself, too.

"Well, get on out there," said Mrs. Maiden. "All of us are pulling for you."

"Yay, Ashley and Dante! You're going to win the whole thing. I saw your dressage score. You're holding first place." Claire, who had ridden Napoleon to the start to see us off, waved our dressage test in the air. The child would not be pried from the pony, but neither could she keep herself from reading the judge's scores and remarks.

"All sevens and eights and even one nine. Listen to this. The judge wrote, 'Exuberant and joyful. Very athletic. Lovely horse; keep him forever,'" Claire read. "You're going to win!"

Napoleon let out the loudest whinny I'd ever heard.

I returned the favor.

John clapped his hands together three times fast. "The ponies are talking to each other. You tell him, Napoleon. Go fast, Dante!" I saw Mrs. Maiden glare at him. "But not too fast."

Ashley gave me leg, and as we were about to enter the starting box, Dana shrieked, "Wait!"

She came running up to us, waving something in her hand.

"You forgot this. Here."

Without Ashley's medical armband, we may not have been allowed on course. The protective vest and the band were easy to ignore, but they served as important reminders that riding cross-country could be dangerous. One slip, one fall, one crash, was all it would take for one or the other of us to get badly hurt. An ambulance and medics were parked right off course, within eyesight, a reminder to me to take every care to bring the girl right back around to home.

With her medical information affixed to her arm, Ashley said, "Thanks, Mom. Love you."

"Me too, you. Hey, have fun."

Ashley nodded. She started back toward the course, but then veered off again. "Whoa."

Her heartbeat and breathing felt normal. I couldn't figure out what might be wrong. Ashley took a big swallow of air and sighed it out long. "Dante, I just want to say thanks."

I sensed some hesitation in her voice.

"See home, way off in the distance?" Something had changed in her. There on the hilltop, it was Ashley who had the look of eagles.

From where we stood, the whole world reflected nothing but mountains in a perfect circle around us. Ashley was right. Due west of where we were standing was the unmistakable double-peaked top of Saddle Mountain, looking every bit like nature's tree-lined expression of a dressage saddle. Just knowing that our hodgepodge of a herd was on the other side, grazing and, I hoped, thinking of us, well, that surely helped to build my confidence.

"Almost every day of my whole life I have seen Saddle Mountain," Ashley said. "I don't know what I'd do without it. Whenever Mom's gone, I miss her so bad. Sometimes, I wake up in the middle of the night and look out my window and ask the mountain to keep her safe. That doesn't make any sense, does it?"

Made perfect sense to me. I myself had taken to doing much the same thing. Wasn't hard to find inspiration and take a lift from all the life in and around the mountain on days when I was feeling too tired and too sore to do much but eat, drink, and rest.

"Anyway, I'm riding for home today, Dante. For all of us. Who are you going for, Monkey?"

She hadn't called me Monkey since the day we met. The affection in her voice circled me up and the moment suspended, as time had on the icy February night of my birth. No fog rolled in and no starry path materialized on the horizon.

But in my knowing eye I saw Marey, Grandfather Dante, Melody, and Filipia. All of them loving me and believing in me. At last, my grandfather's words made sense to me. All of this learning and unlearning and relearning had led me right to three great tests after all: dressage, stadium jumping, and cross-country.

"Sixty seconds," the timekeeper at the starting box said, giving Ashley a warning.

She picked up the reins, and we turned toward the start. Her heart was racing now and mine was following. The cross-country course looked so much bigger than our measly-weasly one at home. The jumps not only looked taller but the terrain was steep and the distance farther than I had gone in a long little while. I danced around and came up off my front feet just a touch. For a jiffy, I panicked. Ashley would be the one who could see the whole course, not me. I'd have to trust her more than I had even trusted Filipia.

"Thirty seconds!" the timekeeper shouted.

Ashley bent forward and whispered to me, "There's a little creek down there for us. Let's go play in the water, Dante."

One mile. Fourteen jumps. Two splashes through water and the entire course unfolding alongside the Maury River, surrounded by our blue mountains.

"Ten, nine, eight!"

It was our time to show up, and our time to win, but I froze.

Now, the Belgian would have thundered down the first hill like a charger into battle. Gwen would've bided her time, set herself up for each obstacle in its right time. Daisy? For sure, she would've paused first to recall an ancient tale about a Celtic pony who flew like an angel over the rough and dangerous landscape. And Napoleon. The little guy would have powered through the course like his life depended on it.

"Seven, six, five, four!"

What would a racehorse do? I asked myself. *Will this OTTB traverse over wide-open land at full throttle just to get through it, come the devil or high water? Or will I give myself over to a full partnership with Ashley?*

"Three, two, one, zero!"

And we were off.

Like I did in my very first race, I stumbled out of the start box. My two front knees grazed the grass, but Ashley lifted my head with the reins and raised herself slightly out of the saddle. "Up, up, up, Dante. Here we go."

She wouldn't let me canter, at first, but posted right purposefully to keep me at the trot. I heard Mrs. Maiden yell, "Good girl, Ashley. Let him settle."

She was riding smart, and I was glad, otherwise my

natural inclination would've whirled us around and raced us back to the trailer.

"Log jump first. Just like home," Ashley said, and we sailed. "Nice." She almost sounded surprised.

We cantered to the rolltop and took it with ease, then Ashley brought me back to the trot again.

As we neared the bottom of the first hill, I caught sight of a brushy spread. Problem was, I couldn't judge how deep it was, and I thought I might fall into a powerful-strong state of colic. A little part of me considered that perhaps if I refused then, maybe Ashley would quit, give up, and we could go home. But I was more afraid to face Daisy than to give it a try.

I had quit on the track many, many times. I wasn't going to quit on Ashley. We might crash the jump, but I was going.

Napoleon whinnied his little heart out. "Lift and hurl, Dante!"

On the approach, Ashley picked up the canter and began counting. "One, two. One, two."

She kept both legs on me, and in the right perfect spot she rose into her two-point.

"Got it! Good boy! Almost to the creek."

With every jump my confidence was growing. I could feel that Ashley's was, too.

We trotted into a cool, shadowy narrow strip of pines, flushing small birds and rabbits as we passed through. As we exited the woodsy part of the course, my eyes needed time to adjust back to the sunshine. Ashley slowed down a bit. Up ahead, I saw the next obstacle: log jump–two strides–log jump. Ashley finally asked for the canter, and she was smiling. I knew why: because I was cantering not galloping, just like she'd asked.

I took a long spot over the first of the two logs in the combination, and Ashley lost a stirrup. She managed to stay on, and we got over the second one clean. She picked up her stirrup and let me run across the flat stretch toward the creek.

"Let's play, Dante! Are you ready?" Ashley dialed me down from a canter to a forward trot through the creek. I flicked my feet to make the water splash us both and I whinnied for more water, but before I could even attempt to misbehave, she flashed her crop.

Once out of the water, the scariest obstacle yet, a stone wall, presented itself on the course. "Nailed it," Ashley said as we popped right over and cantered away.

We rolled back, picked up two more easy fences, and headed toward the creek for our last pass through. This time, I snorted as we got close because I was so happy and the water felt so good.

"Dante, you're crazy." Ashley started grinning and kept on smiling over a brick wall, a variety of brushy verticals, log jumps, and one last combination.

Off in the distance, up near the start, our Maury River Stables family looked small and far away, but I could still hear Napoleon's voice and the cheers of our people, calling our names.

By then, I could feel that Ashley's smile was about to come off her face it was so broad. I got a good spot over the last jump, and we had one thing left to do to finish.

"Run, Dante," Ashley said. "We made it. We're home free."

Ashley didn't need to tell me what to do then. Something shifted in me. Out there with her, everything was open and natural and free, and I was a part of everything. Nothing could stop us, and nothing did.

We crossed the finish line to cheering and jumping and hooting and hollering—the sound of my people feeling happy. Noise I had come to love. Maybe, finally, I had figured out what it means to use your heart.

* CHAPTER FIFTY-TWO *

GHOST HORSE

O r, maybe I hadn't figured out anything at all.

Oh, for sure, over the next two years Ashley and I went on to achieve more than anyone could have expected or even imagined. We rode our way to High-Point Horse and Rider at the Tamworth Springs jumper series. We returned, with confidence and joy, to the Horse Center many a time.

Kentucky Bloodlines even ran a story on OTTBs, featuring yours truly, Dante's Inferno, son of Dante's Beatrice, grandson of Dante's Paradiso. They sent a reporter all the way to Saddle Mountain to meet and photograph me. That picture, all framed and pretty, now hangs inside Mrs. Maiden's office with a golden plaque bearing my name.

Heck, we even caravanned to Riverside once when they held an OTTB festival to raise funds for the retired racehorse program. My friend John did not join us, but he asked me all about it later.

Life was, as they say, good.

Success must be a funny, fickle prize. When you think you've got it, well, that's exactly when you don't. The year I turned ten was the year I learned that as far as I had come, I had that much farther to go.

The real test of my life arrived then. A new horse.

No, not a new horse. An old one. An old, broken-down, going-blind, half-starved all-white Appaloosa without spots showed up to the Maury River Stables in a trailer.

His name was Take-A-Chance; Chancey, they called him. And that's what Mrs. Maiden decided to do. She hadn't the heart to send him away, which is exactly what I would have done.

I thought he was too far gone to be of any use or any good to anybody. For two seasons prior, Chancey had been abandoned in a field with no hay, no shelter but for cedar trees, and no water in his tub. Left to die or survive on his own, it seemed. Struggling through barbed wire to reach the Maury River he had cut up his face and legs and entire body. His ribs protruded and his eyes hollowed.

And I, the horse with the largest of hearts, couldn't stand to look at him. Couldn't stomach his aging smell or tolerate his feeble voice.

To me, Chancey was no longer a horse. He was a ghost. A lingering reminder that no horse is truly his own horse, and every horse is a dependent.

Chancey was not a testament to trust but to fear, the great fear stored away deep inside each equine: that we will become too much of a burden for our people to carry. That our people will, in the end, forsake us.

If Chancey thought life before the Maury River Stables was hard, life was about to get harder.

Because of his weak blue eyes and the damage that the sun did to his pale pink skin, Mrs. Maiden instructed that on turnout Chancey should always wear a fly mask for protection. Napoleon panicked at the thought of the old horse walking around in the dark. He took to pulling the mask off, and I let him.

The boarders chased the App around the field, much as they had chased me when I first came. As they did Mac, when he arrived, too. But Chancey wasn't young like the two of us were. Wasn't strong like us.

When they chased him and bit him and kicked

him, Chancey squealed and whinnied for help, but no help came.

The truth is, not only the boarders treated him cruelly and wanted him gone.

I confess.

I admit.

I ask forgiveness, for I participated. I have no excuse save that his condition and his presence frightened me, because he could have been me or Macadoo or any one of us, mares or geldings.

Looking back, I imagine there were times Chancey wished that he had been left alone in his field after all. Except, I imagine wrongly.

Despite my own abhorrence of Chancey, Claire loved him with all her heart. And he loved her back. In time, Gwen and Macadoo came to Chancey's defense, too, in a way that no horse had ever come to mine. Add jealousy to my sins against him.

What they saw in him, what Claire and Mrs. Maiden saw in him, I did not see.

He had no papers. He was vacant. He hadn't grace or beauty or speed. He did nothing but take up space and eat our hay.

When Mrs. Maiden rearranged our stalls and situated Chancey beside me, I protested the decision mightily all through the first night — and the second. I kicked our shared wall nonstop, so that I wouldn't have to listen to Chancey's labored breathing, reminiscent of the lame mare who had arrived at Riverside with me and was gone by morning. I kicked out so that I wouldn't have to watch him wince and pace as so many I had met in my racing days, those for whom pain and suffering was a way of life till there was no more life.

The old App had come limping into my wildly successful life, dragging the real past and imagined future. I couldn't abide it. I did not consider Chancey one of mine to protect. I wanted him gone.

I confess.

I admit.

I was wrong.

For two nights, I kicked and threatened Chancey through the bars. On the third night, the old App placed a mouthful of grain on the ledge between our stalls.

"Here. I'm growing stronger every day. This is for you. I don't need it."

Chancey stood still and watched while I ate it.

"Someday, you can repay me," he said.

I turned away.

The old App and I always kept some space between us. He did grow stronger, and many came to believe him beautiful. Mrs. Maiden and Mac and Gwen trained him to join the therapeutic school. I watched, incredulous that he could be so still and that for some students stillness, not speed, was exactly what they needed.

I had conquered the three tests of eventing time and time again. I had surrendered my heart to Ashley and joined with a herd. A greater test awaited.

On a cold, snowy afternoon at a time after Chancey's eyesight had completely left him in the dark, Claire took him up Saddle Mountain. She was grieving the loss of a friend, and her heart needed the solid presence of the old App. He did as he was asked to do. He carried Claire across the frigid Maury River and up the mountain, where he stood with her while she grieved. They returned at nightfall, and again, though many years later, Chancey was led into the stall next to mine.

He was cold, shivering, and consumed all his grain and hay in an instant. He asked me for not a thing. The choice was mine to turn away or to recognize Chancey as my brother.

I placed two mouthfuls of grain on the ledge between us.

"Here. I don't need this."

Chancey ate, and I gave him more.

"Thank you," he said. "You are a true friend, Dante."

In that moment, I realized that if the old App was, indeed, a reflection of my future course, as I had once feared, well, I should be so blessed.

CHAPTER FIFTY-THREE

A THOROUGHBRED REVOLUTION

S ome say the fate and fortune of every Thoroughbred boils down to the alchemy of bloodlines. Centuries of mixology endeavoring to produce one horse that will race and win, all for riches and fame or plain old bragging rights.

My own pedigree begins with my dam and my sire, then spirals back through the ages to the three stallions of the Orient: the Byerley Turk, the Darley Arabian, and the Godolphin Arabian.

Some say the original stallions were stolen. Others swear they were gifted by men of wealth and power in the East to men of equal wealth and power in the West. Either way, the founding sires tasted the salt of the sea as they journeyed to the British Isles, where the lost mares of Great Britain brought size and strength and heart into the family. Together they made history by creating a new breed, my breed, the Thoroughbred. Every Thoroughbred heart since the merger of the three Eastern stallions with the English mares has beat for the sake of winning races.

But all that might be changing.

I imagine that Grandfather Dante understood the changes facing our breed. I reckon that's why he called to me from across the ancestral plain.

For the longest time, I misunderstood what Dante's Paradiso meant when he told me that our breed needed a new kind of champion. When he described to me the three great tests and urged me to use my heart, I could not comprehend his meaning. Not until I had lived the journey.

What Grandfather Dante knew long before I did was that there are many more losers than winners at the track. Like me. Legions never even get to put hoof to the dirt that will lead but one to the winner's circle.

Just what happens to all these Thoroughbreds who never race or never win—and to those who win big, but for whatever reason aren't selected to continue the bloodlines?

After all — just ask Chancey — horses can live thirty years. Or longer. And that's a fact.

If you're me, with my pedigree, my training, my grandfather's striking good looks and large heart, and my dam's intelligence, science says you've got it all, you're destined for the history books as a great race-horse and nothing less. But don't bet the barn on what science predicts, because life may hold other adventures, and the science of the heart is not the same thing as the spirit of the heart.

Every horse has his own race to run. For sure, neither fame nor fortune is the destiny of everyone. In my case, Marey surely did try to ease me out of my stubborn willfulness and into the mold of a champion racer. As it happens, I discovered that my heart was not made for the track, after all.

I can recall my sour old trainer, Gary, explaining his disappointment in me: "Even the best-regulated families will throw a dud now and again."

By dud, he meant me.

I was born on February fourteenth; an ironic beginning for a horse who would end up needing years and more years to learn what it means to use your heart. Maybe the clue lives in those wise words of Filipia's Melon: *God's greatest act was to make one day follow another.* If that's so, then I reckon that the greatest act of my heart in response is to rise each new day and try again to offer my best.

But to those who say the fate of every Thoroughbred comes down to pedigree, I say, no, our fate is sealed by the heart. And I say, now is the time for a new kind of champion. Now is the time for a Thoroughbred revolution, and I *am* just the horse to lead it.

Thank You

While I was writing *Dante,* we lost our dear Albert, who inspired *Chancey of the Maury River.* Thank you to all of my readers who asked about him and comforted us after he left this old world. We recently brought a little paint pony named Angel into our family. She truly lives up to her name. Albert and Angel impressed many a hoofprint onto this story.

I thank my generous friend Meg Medina, who helped me to imagine the jockey Filipia.

Much love and gratitude to these horses for their inspiration: My Sweet Albert, Angel Sent From Above, Norman, Payita Mia, Morning Latte, Personal Keepsake, Valentina, Pete, Moo, and Dartanian.

Thank you to these good people: Jennifer Wright, DVM, and the folks at 3 Oaks Equine; everyone at Campbell Springs Farm; and the superheroes— equine and human—at the James River Thoroughbred Retirement Foundation. I especially thank Mrs. Nellie Mae Cox, who shared her passion for and knowledge of the amazing Thoroughbred breed.

Thanks also to the James River Writers community. Thank you to my extraordinary agent, Leigh Feldman. Thanks a bunch to my excellent early readers: Judith Amateau, Bella Stevens, and Elena Zerkin.

Thank you to the awesome Candlewick Press team: Maggie Deslaurier, Angela Dombroski, Kate Herrmann, Katie Ring, Rachel Smith, and a duo I love very much: Kate Fletcher and Karen Lotz.

To my generous, loving family: Mom, Mary, Leigh, John, Betty, and always, Bubba and Judith.

Step back inside
the Maury River Stables:

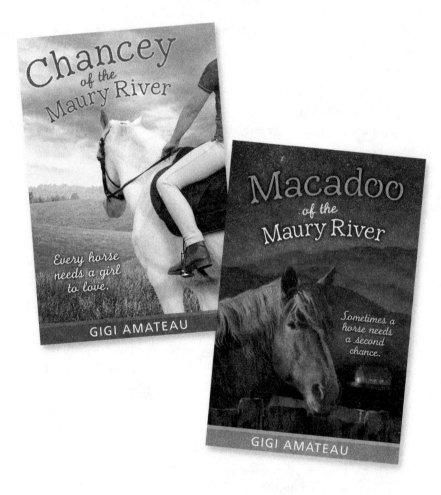

Available in hardcover, paperback, and audio and as e-books.